KU-194-287

JULIE WESTAWAY

"You don't say very much, Julie."

Julie Westaway

by Margaret Barry

Cover and frontispiece by L. F. Lupton

KINGFISHER BOOKS
5 WIGMORE STREET, LONDON, W.1

© Copyright 1958 by Kingfisher Books

First published October 1958

Printed in Great Britain by Richard Clay and Company, Ltd.,
Bungay, Suffolk

CHAPTER ONE

THERE were bright early dahlias in the big brass bowl which stood beside Miss Levering's door. Julie scarcely noticed them. She looked not at the flowers but at the bowl itself, at the intricate leaf design with which it was decorated, and at the shining, lustrous polish which was her own particular pride. At that moment it seemed to her the symbol of all that she was about to leave.

No other person at the Roselinden Home for Girls had so close an acquaintance with the brass bowl as did Julie Westaway. Friday by Friday, leaf after leaf, for almost four years she had brought it back to brilliance with skilful hand and polishing cloth; but now she would do it no more. She wondered who would do it in her place. Miss Blake had always been so particular about those special bits of brass. Julie sighed. After twelve years she was going to miss Miss Blake.

The two girls who shared the long seat with her giggled and twisted. Julie wished that they wouldn't. She was quite sure that neither of them could be as inwardly nervous as she, for both had relatives of a sort, and therefore the pattern of their future lives had some kind of certainty about it. It was customary for girls to go to their relatives when the time came for them to leave Roselinden. Julie herself had no-one. Her father's second wife couldn't be counted. *She* had washed her hands of Julie years before, when she had married someone else. The Roselinden authorities had looked everywhere, but nowhere could they find a trace of even one person who in any way belonged to Julie Westaway.

"Be sensible, Adrienne," Julie said with the sharpness born of an urgent situation. "There may be someone in with Miss Levering who wants to see you."

It was the wrong approach. Adrienne, already strung up to the highest pitch at the rather remote possibility of confronting a would-be employer in Miss Levering's office, burst into tears.

"They can't make me go where I don't want to go," she quavered. "Gran said she'd get me a job in the chain stores. I won't go anywhere else."

Across Adrienne's head Julie looked at Lexie Carter. They knew all about Adrienne.

"You'll go where you're told," she said flatly. She fixed her eyes on the brass bowl and on the intricate ornamentation which she had polished so many times for the simple reason that she had had no other choice. "We all will."

She wished immediately that she hadn't added that. It put her on an equal footing with Adrienne Lewis and Lexie Carter. She liked Lexie and had already promised to write to her; but Roselinden had its own social distinctions—the tinies, the little girls, the big girls—and for two years Julie had been in a class of her own because of her age. It was most unusual for a girl to remain at the Homes for more than a few months after her fifteenth birthday. It had only been because of Julie's complete lack of family ties and her extreme usefulness that the directors, in a time of acute staff shortage, had decided to hold her at Rose-linden for another year or two.

At the time Julie had been utterly grateful. The thought of going out alone into the world appalled her still, and now, waiting with Adrienne and Lexie for the word which would determine the entire course of her future, she could only wish that all this suspense had been over and done with two years before. She felt curiously alone. She had grown away from girls of her own age. No, that wasn't right. They had grown away from her. It was she who had been left isolated.

The office door opened and Miss Levering stood there, tall, trim, perfectly groomed, at once approach-able and aloof. "Adrienne, please," she said in the crisp, clear voice which could administer praise or rebuke with little variation of expression.

The chair facing Miss Levering's desk was unoc-cupied. It was quite apparent that no unknown person was there. Adrienne gulped and got to her feet. The door closed behind her.

"I expect she'll go to live with her grandmother," Lexie whispered, nervously tracing an imaginary out-line on the good plain carpet with the toe of her shoe. "I wouldn't like to have to go and live with *her*, would you, Julie?"

"No," said Julie decisively. Adrienne's grandmother was one of the oddities of the monthly visiting-day at Roselinden. But she was faithful, and at least she was *someone.* Julie sighed. It was even possible that poor little Adrienne was fond of her grandmother.

Lexie wriggled. "I'm pretty sure I'll go to live with Alice," she said. She had said it, to herself, to anyone else who would listen, ever since Miss Blake had told her of the summons to Miss Levering's office. "Alice is quite nice, really. I think I'd rather live with her than go to a hostel. Miss Blake said a hostel is something like this but I'd have to look after myself. I would at Alice's, too, of course. She says she's never finished, with four children, and after all she's only a cousin, and Miss Blake says it wouldn't do to expect too much." She paused, and the silence where her voice had been seemed almost visible. "It's quiet up here, isn't it?" she whispered.

"Yes." Julie had already heard every detail of the possibility of life with Alice. Lexie had even gone so far as to give her Alice's address. "Yes, I hope you *will* go to Alice. Yes, it *is* quiet up here. It gives you time to think," she added pointedly.

It gives you something to think about, too, she told herself. She had been looking back over twelve years, seeing herself waiting, on rare and supremely important occasions, on this very seat with the quaint carved ends; entering the very door which had just closed behind Adrienne, seeing Miss Levering, always trim, always beautifully correct, behind her desk; hearing Miss Levering's crisp, clear voice as it broke the news which was, each time, to have so marked an influence on her life.

Her memory of the first occasion was indistinct.

She knew that her mother had died and that her father, stern and remote in his Air Force uniform, had brought her to Roselinden because there was no other place for a little girl of five who had no-one to look after her. She had only the vaguest memories of her mother. Her voice had been soft, Julie remembered, but perhaps that was because she had been so sick for so long. She knew now that the Second World War had been in progress when her mother died.

She had been six when Miss Levering told her about the new mother. She could not remember how she had felt about that. The deepest impression was made by Miss Levering's assurance that, once the war was over, her father and his new wife would make a home together and would take Julie to live with them. Julie, though happily installed at Roselinden, liked the idea of that. It had been easy to like Hazel. Hazel had insisted on the Christian name from the beginning. Looking back, Julie was grateful for that. She could never have called Hazel by the name of 'Mother'. She accepted Hazel as a new friend, and it gave her tremendous pleasure to look forward to Hazel's appearance on visiting days. Against her father's quietness, his cold, untouchable reserve, Hazel's easy friendliness was as the warmth of sudden sunshine, and her vivid prettiness was that of a brilliant butterfly against a sombre background. But the home together never materialised. It was less than a year later that Miss Levering broke the news of Pilot-Officer Westaway's death in an aeroplane disaster.

Julie remembered that occasion very clearly. She

was now an orphan, Miss Levering said, and Roselinden would be her permanent home until she was fifteen. Her stepmother would continue to visit her, but, so far as a home was concerned, there was no place other than Roselinden.

She had been nine when she received the blow that was, in its own way, the heaviest of all. Her stepmother, the one person to whose affection she had any real claim, and who had been as faithful in her visits as the closest relative could have been, deserted her. Miss Levering didn't put it just like that, of course. She had explained it all very nicely. Mrs. Westaway was to be married again, she was going away to live at some distance, she would no longer be able to visit Julie. The fact that Hazel did not so much as come to say good-bye hurt Julie terribly.

At fifteen her life was so closely woven into the life of Roselinden that she felt herself a part of it. Cottage Two was her home; its matron, Miss Blake, and its thirty girls formed her family circle. She had no clear recollection of any other way of life, and now she was seventeen, and within one week or perhaps two she would know it no more, this security which was known as Roselinden . . .

Miss Levering's door opened and Adrienne came out.

"I'm going to live with Gran," she said in an almost dazed whisper, as if such a thought had never occurred to her or to anyone else. "Miss Levering thinks Gran is going to get me a job in a delicatessen." She passed on and down the stairs.

"I wouldn't like to work in a delicatessen," Lexie said nervously. "I wouldn't mind being in a grocer's, with everything in packets . . ."

"Alexia, please," said Miss Levering.

Julie was rather glad to be alone. She felt strangely disinterested in her future. It presented such a blank and was so entirely unmarked with visible possibilities that it was useless even to guess, though she did share Lexie's feelings about the delicatessen. She hoped Lexie would be happy. She was the one girl of the younger age group to whom Julie felt personally drawn.

Julie looked around her. So much of Roselinden had not changed since she first sat, small and silent, beside her father on this self-same seat. The carpet was new. Julie could remember when its plain costliness had replaced the old flowered one which had been worn by so many feet. The walls had been freshly painted, but nothing else had been changed. The big brass bowl had always been there, and the picture of old Mr. Rose, the founder of the Homes, in its handsome frame; and, hanging above the door of Miss Levering's office, there still remained the shabby, inartistic, cardboard text which was destined, because of Mr. Rose's express wish, to retain this place of honour so long as Roselinden continued to open its doors to homeless little girls.

Julie looked hard at it. She rather thought that, if Miss Levering had had her way, it would have been taken down and hidden away in a drawer long ago. Miss Levering liked everything to be just so. There had been a time when Julie had only been able to pick out a word of the text here and there, but now she could repeat it with her eyes shut.

"My God shall supply all your need according to His riches in glory by Christ Jesus." Phil. 4. 19.

She smiled, remembering how surprised she had been to discover that Phil. meant the same as Philippians in the Bible which Miss Blake had given to her, according to the rules of Roselinden, on her eighth birthday. Miss Blake had told her the story of the text, too. Miss Blake had been at Roselinden for thirty years. She could even remember old Mr. Rose.

Mr. Rose and his wife had been a very ordinary couple of modest means. They had a nice little home and would have been perfectly happy but for one thing. They were both passionately fond of children; yet they were childless. They sometimes talked about adopting a little girl—Mr. Rose adored little girls—but it was not until they were well past middle-age that a suitable opportunity came and they took Belinda, then two years of age, into their home. They almost worshipped Belinda in the three years that they had her, and then she was stricken with some nameless disease for which, in those days, there was no known remedy and, almost without warning, Mr. and Mrs. Rose found themselves childless again.

It was a heartbreaking experience and one from which they might never again have lifted their heads but for a most amazing happening which turned their thoughts from themselves. A scarcely-known relative died, leaving his large and comfortable home, in its pleasant and spacious grounds, to Mr. Rose. An idea, born in his heart and nourished in his mind, lifted Mr. Rose's thoughts beyond himself and his sorrow. The big house would be an ideal haven for several little girls who, like Belinda, had no home to call their own.

Mr. Rose had a big house and a big heart but very little money. He went to one friend after another, but his friends were caught up with their own affairs. He went to the few wealthy business men he knew, but they were too cautious, too hard-headed to see the vision which he had seen. He went to his church, to his lawyer and to every remote member of his own family, but there was no-one who could help him. He had almost given up the idea when someone told him of two little girls who needed just such a home. Mr. Rose was not a young man, but there was fighting blood in his veins and he determined that he would not be beaten. His heart rose to the challenge.

The text came into the story at this point. Miss Blake said there were two versions of what happened: some said that Mr. Rose had opened his Bible at Philippians 4 and the verse had shone out as if in letters of gold; others that a minister had preached on it in the hour of Mr. Rose's deepest need. In any case, it had made a profound impression on Mr. Rose. In his venture of faith he could find no-one to help him but God. Very well. He would turn to God. Miss Blake had made it sound as if God was the very last resort.

Mr. Rose sold his own modest home and moved his few belongings to the big one. Mrs. Rose had hunted through the book-shops until she found a cardboard text with the right words and they hung it in the place of honour over the mantelpiece in the dining-room. Between them they somehow contrived to take not only the two waiting little girls into their home but another and then another. And, all the time, through all their difficulties, God *did* supply all their modest needs. And then, quite suddenly, things changed. People became interested. Money came in from the very business men who had previously refused it. The neighbouring churches caught the vision and rallied to the task. Mr. Rose's worries were over. Roselinden was soundly established, quickly expanded, periodically remodelled and enlarged; instead of one house there were six, and, even before the death of Mr. Rose, Roselinden was famous.

Suddenly something about that story met something that was in Julie's mind. Mr. Rose, in his time of need, had turned to God. He and Mrs. Rose had been alone, quite alone, when they stepped out into the biggest thing in their lives. She, Julie Westaway, would be alone, quite alone, when she stepped out from the shelter of Roselinden into a life which was frighteningly unknown. Mr. Rose had turned to God and He had supplied all his need. Julie knew that she couldn't expect God to do that for *her*. Mr. Rose had turned to God because he knew where to find Him. In that moment Julie knew that *she* didn't. She and God had never become really acquainted. She doubted if He would even recognise her name . . .

The office door opened. Lexie came out, her eyes shining.

"To Alice," she breathed. "I'm going to learn dress-making."

Julie sat very still. The time had come. She had no Gran, no Alice. She didn't even have God. While she had had Roselinden she had had no need of God. Now . . .

Miss Levering's voice came, calm, impersonal.

"Julie, please."

CHAPTER TWO

In twenty years at Roselinden Miss Levering had seen countless girls come and go. Her work this morning was of a routine nature and excited in her no particular feeling. Miss Levering had never permitted herself to become fond of the girls. She put a neat tick beside the name of Alexia Carter.

She felt that she had done all that was possible for Alexia. The girl had a knack with her needle and was sufficiently intelligent and persevering to make good, and her cousin would be a conscientious guardian. Yes, it was a satisfactory arrangement, and Alexia would reflect credit on her Roselinden upbringing. *That* was the important thing.

Adrienne Lewis need not be given another thought. She would be in the hands of her grandmother, and it was Miss Levering's opinion that Adrienne was unlikely to make a success of anything. Roselinden would make the usual parting gift of a new outfit and would then consider its job well done.

She looked now at Julie Westaway, standing straight and slim before her in the grey linen uniform, with the embroidered rose on the pocket, which had been designed by Miss Levering herself. The roses, she felt, had been a clever touch—pink ones for the tinies, red for the little girls, a deep, rich yellow for the older ones. None but Miss Levering could have designed such a delicate compliment to the founder of Rose-linden. She had sometimes been a little dubious about the choice of grey for the uniforms, but she noticed now that it suited Julie very well, with her fair colouring and darker grey eyes and her natural dignity. Julie was different from the other girls. For several reasons Miss Levering had always considered Julie's a most unusual case. Few girls were so entirely destitute of family ties.

"Sit down, Julie, please," she said quietly. "I believe I have been able to make a very happy arrangement for you."

Miss Levering took up her pen and laid it down again. She felt almost ill at ease. Julie was not a child, and somehow she had contrived to keep so much expression from her face that Miss Levering had the curious feeling that the girl's reserve was almost equal to her own.

"You will go to live with Mrs. Loch," she said.

"Yes, Miss Levering," said Julie obediently. She waited. She knew no Mrs. Loch.

"There was a time, Julie, when there would have been a waiting list of people who wanted a girl of your capabilities. Your work has always been satisfactory, but Miss Blake tells me that of late years it has been exceptional. Talents vary. We have girls who can sew. Alexia is an example. We have girls who can draw and paint and others who can come top of the class in mathematics. Yours is, perhaps, a rarer talent, Julie. Miss Blake believes that you are a born home-maker."

Miss Levering paused.

"Not many homes are open to girls nowadays. There was a time, as I have said, when I could have placed you in a dozen—a clergyman's home, perhaps. But things have changed, and most people have installed more and better labour-saving devices and prefer to look after their own homes. We also have to be particularly careful in your case. You will be a ward of Roselinden for another four years, and we had to find some home which was not too far away for us to keep a watchful eye on your interests. So Mrs. Loch's request for one of our girls was most timely. Mrs. Loch is one of our committee ladies. You may have seen her at some time, Julie."

"I may have," Julie said guardedly. A question was burning on the end of her tongue but she dared not ask it. There were two kinds of committee ladies, the sewing committee and the inspection committee. They were as different as sunshine and shadow. The sewing ladies came every second week, from each of the churches in turn, for Roselinden was the responsibility of none in particular yet made an appeal to all. They were cheerful, chatty folk, pleasant, friendly, finding considerable pleasure and entertainment in darning and patching together. There was nothing awe-inspiring about them, as there was about the inspection ladies, who monthly looked into the cupboards and the stores and made even the experienced Miss Blake a little hard to please on the mornings when they were expected. The sewing ladies came by 'bus, the inspection ladies in sleekly shining cars, and when the weather was even the least little bit chilly they wore fur capes. Julie had come to look upon a fur cape as the badge of a social level infinitely higher than all others. To live with one of the inspection ladies would be quite terrifying, but all the sewing ladies looked as if they would polish their own floors and wash up their own dishes.

"Mrs. Loch lives only a mile from Roselinden," Miss Levering continued. "She has a very lovely home, and she will expect you to keep it in perfect order. You will do your very best, I know."

"Yes, Miss Levering," Julie said mechanically. There was little doubt about it. Mrs. Loch would belong to the fur capes.

"The home is large but the family is small—just Mr. and Mrs. Loch, and their daughter, who is a little older than you." Miss Levering hesitated. It was never easy to tell a girl that the standards of Roselinden and of the outside world were not exactly the same. "You have become a person of some importance here, Julie. To the younger girls you are virtually a grown-up. To the older girls you are a big sister. I think you will understand that your position in Mrs. Loch's household will be entirely different. Her daughter, though a girl of much your own age, will be on the same level as her mother so far as you are concerned. Her name is Marguerite, but you will be expected to call her Miss Loch."

Julie nodded. Miss Blake was rigidly old-fashioned in some ways, and stern lessons in respect and good manners had been taught since the day of Julie's arrival at Roselinden. She had seen little enough of the outside world, but she had no difficulty in picturing the daughter of a fur-caped mother. She seemed even more alarming than the mother herself. Julie would overstep no bounds of decorum *there*. Miss Levering could be very sure of that.

"You will commence your duties on the first of February. Mrs. Loch will call to see you to-morrow. Be here at ten sharp, Julie. I will send a note to Miss Blake. That is all, except—Julie, I want to ask you a question. You have never had any word or sign from your stepmother, have you?"

"No, Miss Levering."

"Think hard, Julie. It is eight years since she last came to see you. In all that time someone might possibly have brought you a message from her. You don't even know where she lives?"

"No, Miss Levering."

"I just wanted to be satisfied on that point. She is not likely to contact you now, after so many years." Miss Levering had long ago discovered (for Miss Levering had ways and means of discovering most things) that Hazel had made a very poor second marriage and was living in one of the least desirable suburbs of Sydney, but she did not mention those things to Julie. Miss Levering, experienced student of human nature, had seen Hazel for what she was—a pretty, shallow girl who had been married by a desperately lonely man in a time of national emergency when nothing seemed to matter. She was of the brightness that quickly dims, the cheapness that reveals itself on closer acquaintance, and Miss Levering could not but feel that things had worked out for the best, so far as Julie was concerned.

"That leaves you, as we thought, entirely without even remote family connections. The directors and I have made every possible enquiry. Westaway is not a common name. Nor was your mother's maiden name. Yours is a solitary position, Julie, but you must never think of yourself as being altogether alone."

Miss Levering paused significantly. She was about to say something of extreme importance. For a moment Julie thought that she might be going to speak about God. But that moment passed. Miss Levering wasn't going to *that* extreme.

"Roselinden will always be here," Miss Levering said. "And now you may go and tell Miss Smythe that I am ready to deal with the mail."

Julie imparted the news to Lexie as they shelled the peas together. Lexie was impressed. She had the greatest respect for the inspection committee, and, while she would have been petrified with fright at the thought of going into the home of one of the ladies herself, she had superb confidence in Julie's ability to grace any establishment. She dismissed lightly the thought of Miss Marguerite Loch.

"She won't be as nice as you, Julie," she said loyally. "You'll write and tell me every single thing, won't you? I did give you Alice's address, didn't I?"

"I'm sure you did. Forty-five Waterside Crescent. You'll like being near the beach, Lexie. I wish I could have a day there with you sometimes."

Miss Blake was also impressed but more cautious. She had done her very best with Julie, and never had she had so responsive a pupil, but that difficult Mrs.

Loch might expect the impossible. Miss Blake recalled one or two searching questions about the contents of her own immaculate cupboards.

"You must have seen her, Julie," she said. "A dumpy little woman with only the shape that you buy in shops, but as condescending as a duchess. I've seen the house, too, as it happens. It's an old-style two storey place—Early Colonial, I suppose you'd call it. I daresay it would be considered *old*, as Australian houses go." Miss Blake, who was English born, had never really forgiven Australia for being such a young country. "It has style, I'll grant you. You're really very fortunate, Julie. It isn't every girl who has her needs met in this way."

Something about the words was familiar but Julie did not follow the thought. Her mind was on the awesome Mrs. Loch.

"I expect she'll be very particular, Miss Blake."

"You'll learn a lot," said Miss Blake succinctly.

"I expect the daughter will be very sophisticated."

"Couldn't be otherwise, with *her* mother. Are those peas ready, girls?" Miss Blake sighed. It would be easy enough to find someone else to shell the peas, but she just couldn't imagine how she'd get along without Julie in a host of other ways. She laid a hand on the girl's shoulder.

"You can always come back and ask me anything you're not sure about," she said. "And I don't think you need bother yourself about the daughter, Julie. You'll see little enough of *her*."

CHAPTER THREE

AT ten minutes to eleven, on the morning of the first of February, Mrs. Philip Loch assured herself that all was ready for the coming of Julie Westaway. The little room at the end of the hall upstairs was in flawless order. She had furnished it especially — not expensively, for that, she thought, would not have been in the best of taste—and the pale pink of the walls went perfectly with the deeper pink of the draperies and contrasted delicately with the three chalk-white roses in the blue bowl on the skirted dressing-table. It was exactly as Mrs. Loch wished Julie to keep it. Rose-linden standards were high, but the standards of Mrs. Loch were higher. She rather wished that Marguerite hadn't hung that calendar on the wall. It looked a little out of place, and the child mightn't care for that sort of thing. . . .

There were dainty egg-and-lettuce sandwiches in readiness for morning tea, and the second-best china was on the traymobile. It was important that Julie should see, from the beginning, that all niceties must be observed. There was nothing more which could be done. Mrs. Loch chose the glossiest magazine from the rack and sat down to idle away the ten minutes with it. She had done everything possible. No-one could have done more.

It occurred to her, as she turned the second page

of the magazine, that she hadn't looked in on Marguer
ite's room, but Marguerite had promised to have every
thing just right and with that she must be satisfied
although she feared that her daughter was just a *little*
casual when it came to orderliness. She did not fee
like going upstairs again just to make sure. There
would be no need for Julie to enter Marguerite's room
to-day, and, although she scarcely liked to admit i
even to herself, Mrs. Loch had found just recently
that the stairs were beginning to worry her. That wa
one of the reasons why she was glad to be bringing
Julie Westaway into the home.

That, and Marguerite. She wasn't happy about
Marguerite. She'd come away from school with such
odd ideas. Marguerite's education had been something
on which Mrs. Loch and her husband had not agreed,
and now she felt that her judgment, though over-
ruled, had been proved correct. It had been her sole
desire that Marguerite should attend an expensive
school of the highest social standing. Philip could
afford it. There was no question of that. But Philip
had been adamant. The local co-educational High
School, where tuition was free, had an excellent repu-
tation. Only the top pupils of the district were admitted. Her father had been justly proud when Marguerite
gained entrance. That, he said, was something that
money couldn't buy. He turned a kindly but deaf ear
to his wife's objections on the score that Marguerite
would be mixing with all the wrong sort of people.

Mrs. Loch had never reconciled herself to the situation. Marguerite had done well, scholastically. Her

pass in the Leaving Certificate Examination had been highly creditable. She had matriculated with honours, and a wide range of professions was open to her. But Mrs. Loch was not happy about her.

"She has formed friendships which are not within the right circle," she told her husband. "She looks at things from a most extraordinary angle—religion, in particular—and if she goes straight on to University I am afraid that I shall have no influence whatsoever over her. I want to have her to myself for a year, Philip. I can take her to the right places, introduce her to the right people. Please try to see my point of view. At the end of the year she can decide for herself."

Surprisingly, although he could not see his wife's point of view, he had agreed. Marguerite was as gay as a lark; therefore she must be happy, and that was the thing that mattered. Gwendoline was inclined to take an extreme view of things, he thought tolerantly. He had made one stipulation.

His wife must be free to come and go as she wished, for Marguerite's sake; but it was essential, for his own sake, that no change be made in the routine of his home life. He was a busy man, and only the excellence of Mrs. Loch's kitchen organisation had enabled him to cope with all his responsibilities. Meals must be on time; it would be necessary, if Mrs Loch were to feel really free, to employ permanent help in the home. And so it was arranged that Julie Westaway, who had not a soul in the world who belonged to her, should come . . .

A quiet little thing, Mrs. Loch thought, turning the pages of her magazine without seeing a thing that was there. Quiet, and either nicely-mannered or too shy to be herself in the brief interview which they had had in Miss Levering's office. Mrs. Loch believed that she would fit in very nicely, and both Miss Levering and Miss Blake had praised her work—almost *too* highly, Mrs. Loch felt. They had almost made it appear that Roselinden and Julie were bestowing a favour on Mrs. Loch.

At three minutes to eleven the telephone rang sharply beside her. She was used to telephone calls, from people asking her advice about some committee matter or the other, perhaps asking her to judge a cooking competition at a church bazaar or even inviting her to take the chair at some special women's function. "YC7698. Mrs. Loch speaking," she said crisply.

It was a committee worry, and a complicated one. The secretary of one of Mrs. Loch's pet charity organisations had a grievance which, in Mrs. Loch's opinion, was not justified. She was endeavouring to sift things out with her usual competence when a ring at the front door announced the arrival of Miss Blake and Julie.

Mrs. Loch was not pleased. She was caught at a disadvantage. She had reached a most critical point in her judgment and could not leave the conversation just where it was. She asked the caller to hold the line and, with the utmost dignity, she went to the front door.

Mrs. Loch would have been horrified had she heard

Miss Blake's recent description of her. Short she was, but that was how the Creator had intended her to be, and in her own opinion at least she knew that the fact that she was Mrs. Philip Loch added inches to her height. Plump she also was, but she felt that that was more suited to the dignity of middle-age than Miss Blake's gaunt angularity. She extended a gracious hand, for this was an occasion.

"Would you come in, please?" she said in the tone which Miss Blake would have described as condescending. "I must ask you to excuse me for a moment. I am busy with a telephone caller. Miss Blake, would you take this chair, please? Julie——"

She paused. She had one terse thing to say to the woman on the 'phone, and it was best that Julie should not hear it. She motioned towards the luggage, the new and shining suitcase which contained the new outfit which was always Roselinden's parting gift to its girls, the shabby overnight bag which Miss Blake had lent for the accumulation of oddments which wouldn't fit in elsewhere.

"Perhaps you would like to carry them upstairs, Julie," she said in a voice which turned a suggestion into a command. "You will find my daughter in the second room on the right. She will show you where to put them. Come down as soon as you have disposed of them, please."

Never had stairway seemed so long, or, on the other hand, so short. Each step was a mile, a mile farther from Roselinden, from Miss Blake, from the only home that Julie had ever known. Yet, all too soon, she was

nearing the top, around the curve which hid from
sight the entrance-hall below, where Miss Blake in her
grey Roselinden uniform sat stiffly on an elegant rosewood chair. A sense of utter desolation swept over
her. She was neither upstairs nor down; she belonged,
in that moment, to neither the life behind nor the life
before her. And she was alone.

She remembered what Miss Blake had told her about
old Mr. Rose. When there was no-one else to help him
he depended upon God. But it must have been different
for old Mr. Rose. He must have *known* God, must have
been really acquainted with Him, to be so sure that
He would stand by him in the time of need. You only
felt like that about people you really knew—Miss
Blake, for instance, or loyal little Lexie . . . .

She reached the top and looked around her. It was,
as Miss Blake had said, a lovely home, but she saw
nothing of it but the door of the second room on the
right, and that door was shut. She must knock. Her
footsteps on the carpet had made no sound, and Miss
Marguerite Loch, who was behind that door, would
not know that she was coming. Julie stepped forward,
surprised that her legs had still the power of movement in them. This was the worst, the most overwhelming moment of all. And she was alone.

The first door on the right was open and a movement from within caught Julie's attention. It was a
room which, obviously, was not in use. That wasn't
surprising, Julie thought, in a house of such a size with
so small a family. There were none of the usual signs
of occupation. One of the wardrobe doors hung open,

as if someone had come looking for something in a hurry and had failed to close it. The polished dressing-table with the deep mirror was bare, and standing in front of it was a girl.

Miss Blake had, on various occasions, spoken of being rooted to the spot. For the first time Julie felt that she knew just what Miss Blake had meant. She stopped short, unable to move further.

The girl was tall and beautifully proportioned, and there was a winsome charm in her expressive features which outshone mere prettiness. She wore no vestige of make-up, and on her head, with the soft honey-gold curls twisting delicately beneath its brim, was a brown felt hat. A man's hat.

The crown had been pushed into pork-pie shape and with deft fingers the girl was pulling the brim this way and that until it became a graceful frame for her lovely face. She twisted her head, in an effort to see herself from a different angle, and caught sight of Julie. She laughed, put her left hand to her head to steady the hat, and held out the other.

"You must be Julie," she said. "I'm so glad you've come. I really meant to be downstairs to meet you. It just can't be eleven o'clock yet. I haven't even——" She laughed again. "I suppose you've guessed that I'm Marguerite."

Julie had not. But she had to say something. Miss Blake had schooled her well.

"How do you do, Miss Loch," she said mechanically, surprised that the voice which spoke the formal words should sound like her own.

B

Marguerite frowned. She put her free hand on Julie's arm.

"Listen, Julie. I've been through all that with Mummy. We don't quite see eye to eye. But it's all right. Call me Marguerite."

"Yes, Miss Loch," said Julie meekly.

Marguerite turned back to the mirror.

" Am I supposed to show you to your room, Julie? Could you wait just one minute? It might be better if I wear it just the least bit farther back on my head. Like that." She twisted the hat again. "Yes, that's it. Don't you think so? It just occurred to me five minutes ago that this old hat of Daddy's was almost exactly the sort of hat I'll wear when I'm a deaconess."

"A deaconess!" Julie breathed.

She had seen a deaconess once, an earnest, elderly lady who had come to Roselinden to tell the girls about her work in the poorer parts of Sydney. There must be some mistake.

"It's a brownish uniform with a darker brown hat. Like this." Marguerite smiled at her own reflection in the mirror, yet it was as if she saw something invisible and not herself. "Julie, it's almost twelve months since I knew that God was calling me to full-time service. I didn't know, then, what it was that He wanted me to do. I had to wait for Him to show me the way. Just after Christmas I met a deaconess. She had come to Sydney with some children from the Far West of New South Wales—children who hadn't seen the sea, or an electric train, or been on an escalator . . . I knew then what it was that God wanted me to do."

She adjusted the hat ever so slightly on her honey-gold curls. "Mummy isn't very happy about it, I'm afraid. She wants me to go to the University. Julie, did Mummy say anything about morning tea? I'm famished."

"She didn't mention it," said Julie, thankful to be back on more practical ground and to be able to utter even a brief sentence without stumbling over it, yet so fascinated with the amazing things that Marguerite had to say that she almost wanted her to continue. Marguerite must be on even closer terms with God than old Mr. Rose had been.

"We'll go down in a minute. We can put your luggage away later. I wonder—Julie, I'd like to see how it looks from the back. I'll hang on to it just as it is. That's my room next-door. Could you bring my hand-mirror and—yes, two hatpins—you'll find them on the dressing-table."

Julie obeyed. It was such a small thing to do. Full-time service. Just exactly what did that mean? She opened the door of the second room on the right.

CHAPTER FOUR

It should have been a charming room.

Julie's experience of bedrooms had not been entirely confined to the dormitory at Cottage Two. She was well acquainted with Miss Blake's private quarters, which were as austere and neat as Miss Blake herself. She had also done a little visiting. Twice she had been permitted to go to Alice's with Lexie, because she had no-one of her own to visit; once, as a special treat, she had spent a weekend with Miss Blake's married sister, who had taken her around to visit some of Miss Blake's other relatives; several times she, with others of her class, had gone to tea with one of the Sunday School teachers who week by week had come to Cottage Two. But she had never seen a room like this of Marguerite's.

It exceeded the whole sum of her previous experience in its costliness of furnishing, its girlish charm, and its light-hearted, inexcusable disorder. The imagination of Miss Blake, seated so primly on the rosewood chair downstairs, could never have conceived so complete and carefree a muddle. For one moment Julie, educated to the scrupulous orderliness of Roselinden, caught her breath with disapproval—then, for the first of countless times, she began in her own mind to make excuses for Marguerite.

The bed with its dainty linen was rumpled and unmade. A book lay open on the pillow. One cotton frock was flung carelessly over the back of a chair, another on the end of the bed. Obviously Marguerite had had difficulty in deciding what to wear. A tin of delicately-perfumed talcum powder lay cap-less and overturned on the pale green carpet. An untidy pile of music lay on the lovely little writing-desk, some of it open, some with the corners turned back. Marguerite must have been looking for something in a hurry. The dressing-table was strewn from end to end with such a disarray of trifles that Julie was quite sure that no-one could be expected to know just exactly what *was* there. It reminded her of a party game they had once played at Cottage Two on the occasion of Miss Blake's birthday. Some of the girls had fixed a tray with the most amazing collection of oddments you could imagine—you looked at the tray for one minute, then it was taken away and you had to write down as many of the things as you could remember. Marguerite's dressing-table was like that tray. But there was some reason for that, Julie assured herself. Perhaps Marguerite had overslept. Julie remembered one occasion when that had happened to *her*, and no matter how she tried she hadn't been able to make up the lost time. And Marguerite had so much—it would take time to put everything in its proper place. . . . Julie would not admit even to herself that this was the accumulation of days. . . .

She found the hand-mirror and one hatpin. She had no doubt that search would reveal the other, but Marguerite might think her inquisitive if she lingered. She wanted to please Marguerite. Full-time service. What had Marguerite meant? It apparently had some

connection with God, and therefore it was rather
puzzling; but, if it just meant working at one thing
all the time, then Julie had a shrewd suspicion that she
had found *hers*. She would fetch and carry for Marguerite, and she would find her greatest happiness in doing
it. . . .

"Only one?" Marguerite queried, taking the pin and
skewering it deftly through the crown of the brown
hat. "Did you look on the floor, Julie? Things do seem
to scatter themselves, don't they? Yes, I think that's
how it should be. I had an idea that Miss Sanders wore
hers a shade too far forward." She smiled at herself in
the mirror, and again there came into her face that
soft irradiance which suggested some glimpse of the
invisible. "I shall love being a deaconess," she said.

Then she laughed, whipped the hat from her head,
and threw it on the bed. "I'll put it away later," she
said. "Come on, Julie. Let's run your bags along to the
end of the hall and leave them there. Mummy may be
waiting for us."

Mrs. Loch had been waiting for five minutes. This
alone was sufficient to throw a shadow of constraint
over the morning tea table. Mrs. Loch, of course, was
not wearing her fur cape, yet Julie had the instant
impression that it was there just the same, an invisible
mantle adorning her plump shoulders. Julie also knew
that she had learned her first lesson. She might want to
please Marguerite most, but she must please Mrs. Loch
first. She was almost glad when Miss Blake looked at her
watch and bluntly said that it was time for her to go.

Mrs. Loch was graciousness itself. She assured Miss

Blake that Julie would be happy to see her between two and four on any afternoon other than Monday; and Miss Blake, who resented patronage above all things, and who remembered very clearly those questions about her own meticulous cupboards, rather tactlessly said that she only hoped that Julie would be happy. She kissed Julie brusquely but with real affection—she was going to miss the child—and then she turned her steps towards Roselinden. She could do no more for Julie Westaway, and there were thirty other girls in her immediate charge who would be coming in from school, hungry and hurrying, at half-past twelve. She must put her best foot forward.

"Let's go and unpack your bags, Julie," Marguerite said gently. It must be strange to have known only a Home that was spelt with a capital. "I haven't a thing to do this morning and I'd love to help you."

Mrs. Loch had other plans.

"I think Julie would prefer to do that in her own time this afternoon," she said pointedly. "You can just hang up your frocks and slip into something simple, Julie. My daughter and I are going out immediately after lunch, and I should like to explain your duties to you. Marguerite, will you please ring Mrs. Stacey and ask her if she would prefer us to bring sandwiches or savouries?"

It was all very skilfully, very delicately done, but Julie understood. Miss Blake had been right about Marguerite. She'd see little enough of *her*. Mrs. Loch would see to that. Mrs. Loch was not a committee lady for nothing.

The luggage was standing by the door at the end of the upstairs hall, just as Marguerite had left it. The door was closed. Julie had the curious feeling that she should knock before she opened it. It was almost like going into Miss Levering's office and wondering what was in store for her. Julie Westaway, who had shared a dormitory with thirty other girls for all the years that she could clearly remember, was about to become possessed of a room of her own.

The room was small, but fresh and dainty in a very simple fashion. Mrs. Loch had had several of her friends in to see it, and their admiration of the furnishings, and of Mrs. Loch herself, had been more than satisfying. Julie was charmed. Of all colours she loved pink most passionately, and the rose-coloured curtains, the ruffled drapings of the dressing-table, and the little bed daintily spread with a softer pink were as a welcome to a lonely soul. She bent over the chaste white roses in the blue bowl and was faintly disappointed. They had no perfume. And then, on the wall above the neat little writing-desk, she saw the calendar.

It hung slightly off-square and looked as if it had been put there as an afterthought by some hand other than the one which had arranged the room with such artistic precision. Of course—Marguerite. Marguerite had put it there to help and encourage her, yet somehow it depressed her, for the words beneath a very ordinary picture of swans on a lake were the words of Mr. Rose's text.

'My God shall supply all your need according to His riches in glory by Christ Jesus.'

It was all right for Marguerite. She and God were friends. Julie sighed and turned to her shining new suitcase. She shook out her few frocks and hung them tidily in the wardrobe and slipped into one of the plain pastel cottons which Miss Levering had chosen as suitable to her new status. Then she went downstairs, quickly. She must not keep Mrs. Loch waiting again. . . .

It was not until bedtime that she saw Marguerite again.

The afternoon had seemed endless. It had not taken her long to dispose of her few possessions in her room. There was a place for everything—Mrs. Loch had seen to that—and everything was in its place. Julie possessed no ornaments, no photographs, which would have given personality to her little room. There had been no place for such things in the dormitory at Roselinden. There was a small book-rack on the writing-desk. Mrs. Loch had overlooked nothing, as her friends had admiringly assured her. But Julie owned no books. She liked reading, but she had never known enough to win any of the prizes offered by the Sunday School teacher, and there had been no uncles or aunts to send Christmas or birthday presents. She *did* have her Bible, because Roselinden had provided that; but it looked so battered and forlorn and out-of-place, with no other books to keep it company, that Julie put it back into the drawer.

The duties appointed by Mrs. Loch were few and quickly done. It seemed to Julie that everything had already been done. Mrs. Loch had put the casserole

ready for the oven, and the sweet was in the refriger-
ator. She shelled peas and peeled potatoes and almost
prayed that neither the door-bell nor the telephone
would ring. Mrs. Loch had told her what to do in either
event, but she had also told her so many other things
that Julie doubted if she would ever remember which
rule belonged to what. She soon found herself without
occupation.

Her fingers itched to straighten out the confusion
in Marguerite's room, yet something born of her Roselinden training told her that she was not free to do so.
She was glad when Mrs. Loch came home and gave her
instructions regarding the setting of the dinner-table
for two. Marguerite, it appeared, was staying out for
dinner.

Julie prepared for bed early. She had nothing else to
do. Things would be different to-morrow. Mrs. Loch
would keep her busy. When she had some money she
would buy some wool and begin knitting a jumper.
But who would explain the awkward bits of the pattern to her? She had always gone to Miss Blake for
that, or to Lexie. Lexie seemed to know what to do
with any sort of a needle. Lexie would be going to
Alice's to-morrow. Julie pictured her, spending her
last night at Roselinden, sleeping beside the vacant bed
which for years had been Julie's, and suddenly the
thought of her own loneliness was too painful to
be borne. She switched off the light and got into bed
without giving one thought to the Roselinden routine
of first kneeling down and saying what were supposed
to be her prayers.

She had been there only a few minutes when Marguerite came and sat, against all the rules of Cottage Two, on the side of the bed. Julie was glad that she had not switched on the light. A rosy glow from the lighted hall was enough to softly illumine the little room, but not (Julie hoped) to reveal the traces of tears hurriedly mopped-up. "I was tired," she said lamely.

"Of course. I've been wondering about you, Julie. I didn't in the least want to stay at Mrs. Stacey's for dinner. I would much rather have gone to the I.S.C.F. re-union. But Mrs. Stacey insisted." Marguerite pulled a face. "Mrs. Stacey has a son. Mummy admires him very much. His name is Underwood." She wrinkled her nose expressively. "Did you have an I.S.C.F. at your school, Julie?"

"I don't even know what it means," said Julie humbly.

"*Don't* you?" A look came into Marguerite's lovely face, a look which Julie came to recognise as the fore-runner of a crusade. "It's the Inter-School Christain Fellowship," she explained. "It's great, Julie. I was the leader of the girls' I.S.C.F. at High School last year. We had some super times together. Stuart Meredith (I've known him all my life) was the boys' leader the year before. He's doing medicine at the University new. Second-year. He'll be going out to the mission field, of course."

She paused and looked around the dainty room. "Julie, Mummy is going to love you. You're a girl after her own heart. Rightly speaking you're the sort of girl she should have had for a daughter. Not me." She laughed cheerfully. "To-morrow, Julie, if you will help me, I shall turn *my* room into a model of orderliness which Mummy herself would be unable to outdo!"

"I'll do it for you," Julie said eagerly. "Every day. I'd love to. It's—it's the only sort of thing I *can* do," she added.

Marguerite patted the hump in the bed that was Julie's shoulder. "I'm so glad you've come to live with us," she said simply. "Mummy says you haven't any relatives at all. Julie, are you sure? That just doesn't seem possible. Would you like Daddy to make some enquiries? He knows how to pull the right strings in all sorts of places."

Julie shook her head. She had met Mr. Loch at dinner-time. Julie, whose experience had been almost entirely limited to womenfolk, had been too overcome with nervousness to respond to the courteous pleasantries of the big, good-looking business man. She had no doubt whatsoever that he *could* pull strings, but she knew that Roselinden had already pulled them all.

"There isn't anyone," she said steadily. "Miss Levering tried everywhere. I *did* have a stepmother—her name was Hazel——"

"Did she die, Julie?"

"Oh no. She just didn't come any more. There isn't anyone now. There couldn't be."

Marguerite was not convinced. "There's a lovely verse in Psalm sixty-eight. 'God setteth the solitary in families.' He wouldn't have left *you* out, Julie. You must have someone, somewhere." She warmed to the thought. "Let's pray about it, Julie. Let's ask Him to help us to find someone who belongs to you."

'My God,' said the calendar on the wall, 'shall supply all your need . . .'

That *could* mean someone to belong to her, of course. But Julie shook her head again. She could hardly expect even Marguerite's God to do something which Roselinden had failed to do. "There isn't anyone," she repeated.

Marguerite considered for a moment. "What church do you go to, Julie?"

"We had our own chapel at Roselinden. The different ministers used to come. Once a month Miss Blake or someone else on the staff would take the older girls to church at night. Miss Levering used to tell us which church to go to each time and we'd all go together."

"Did you ever go to St. Cuthbert's, Julie? It's a lovely old church—it has everything that a beautiful church should have—stained glass windows and a choir and a most wonderful organ—I *do* love music, Julie. I go there on Sunday mornings with Mummy and Daddy. But at night I go to the little stone church in Deveringham Road. Daddy and Mummy mostly stay at home at night—they go to St. Cuthbert's if they go anywhere, of course. I don't expect you'd know the church at Deveringham Road. It would be a long way from Roselinden. It isn't grand like St. Cuthbert's, but I love it." The radiance came into the girl's face again. "I gave my heart to the Lord at Deveringham Road. You must come there with me sometimes, Julie." She hesitated, wanting to ask one question yet restrained by some innate delicacy from voicing it. "Do you read the Scripture Union notes?" she asked instead.

"I don't know what they are," Julie confessed.

Instantly, in the manner of Mrs. Loch's invisible fur cape at the morning tea-table, the brown felt hat of the deaconess was there on Marguerite's honey-gold curls. She looked around the room.

"I expect you have a Bible," she said.

"Oh, yes. We had prayers in the dining-room every night, before the little ones went to bed. Miss Blake chose a chapter and we read it verse about."

"Did Miss Blake explain it to you?"

"Oh, no." It would never have occurred to Julie that such a burden could be placed on the shoulders of the already overworked Miss Blake.

"Did you always understand it, Julie?" It was the voice of the deaconess, kind but relentless.

"No," said Julie honestly. Understanding hadn't really entered into it. The conducting of evening prayers was one of the principles of Roselinden, as laid down by old Mr. Rose. It had to be done, just as the shabby old text had to remain on the wall outside Miss Levering's office. "No, I didn't understand much of it at all."

"*Daily Bread* will be best," Marguerite said thoughtfully. "You'll like the Scripture Union notes, Julie. They make even the most difficult passages clearer. I'll get some for you when I'm in town with Mummy tomorrow." She got up from the bed. "I must let you get some sleep, Julie. Have you everything that you need?"

An hour later, oblivious of the disorder around her, Marguerite Loch knelt beside the bed over which, a few minutes earlier, she had drawn the sheets and blankets with more haste than care.

'Help me to help her to find you, Lord," she whispered. "And thank you for sending her here."

CHAPTER FIVE

THE Reverend David Sterling polished his shoes vigorously and whistled 'Sun of my Soul' with equal fervour, although it was little past breakfast-time and he could not expect 'the soft dews of kindly sleep' to fall upon him for another twelve hours or so. He didn't want to sleep, either. The sun was shining and he wanted to get out and about. He glanced furtively around. He hoped that his landlady wasn't watching him. He always cleaned his shoes on his feet and that was a habit which greatly displeased her.

She was nowhere in sight. The Reverend David whistled more energetically than ever, replaced the lid on the shoe-polish tin and put it, with the brushes, into the precise spot on the shelf which Mrs. Featherberry had designated for such things. He wanted to please everyone on this bright morning. Mrs. Featherberry was an old dear, really, with the teapot always handy and a most picturesque tendency for darning his grey socks with green wool and his black ones with grey.

The 'Reverend' was in one sense a courtesy title, for he was not yet twenty-two and his full ordination was still a long way off; but it had been necessary for him to don the title, with his clerical collar, when he took up his probationary appointment at Western Vale and, because of the sorry lack of ministerial manpower, was given the entire work of a minister to do. But the 'Reverend' had made all the difference to Mrs. Featherberry. She had the greatest respect for the clergy and she bestowed on him many privileges which would never have been the portion of a plain Mr. She had found it necessary to speak to him, from time to time, for his own good but, she feared, without making the slightest impression; he really was a pig-headed young man, but what else could you expect from anyone with hair as red as his?

The shoe-polishing things were scarcely in place before she appeared.

"You don't make it sound much like a hymn," she said reprovingly.

"Very sorry," apologised David cheerfully and entirely without repentance. "It's this bright and sunny morning, Mrs. Featherberry. It does things to you. We'll try again." He swung even more gaily into the notes of 'Trust and Obey'.

Mrs. Featherberry permitted no smile to soften her disapproving features. "I came to ask if you would be home for lunch, Reverend Sterling," she said primly.

"I expect so. Aspidistra and I have one promised call to make and then we're going adventuring in Crossley Road. Do you know anyone who lives in Crossley Road, Mrs. F.?"

"I know Mrs. McGlynn," said Mrs. Featherberry in a voice of ominous significance. "And I might go so far as to say that it's about time you *did* visit her, Reverend Sterling. One of our best Guild ladies and all, and the children never missing Sunday School. You need to look after your own. And if you would take one word of advice"—her tone implied that this was extremely unlikely—"I would go so far as to suggest that you do not mention that you call your car—what you call her. She'd wonder why, like we all do."

"As I do myself," confessed David humbly. "I also wonder, as doubtless others do, why I ever bought her. Mrs. Featherberry, I shall visit Mrs. McGlynn this very morning, I shall apologise for my most unpardonable neglect of her, and I shall not mention the unmentionable. Do you know anyone else in Crossley Road?"

"The Frosts live next-door to Mrs. McGlynn. I don't know *them*. They're a poor lot. In and out of gaol, he is, and the woman getting around with no shoes on her feet most of the time, and the children looking as if they hadn't had a square meal since they were born. Mrs. McGlynn feels that they are the thorn in the flesh sent to try her." Mrs. Featherberry sighed dolefully.

"It sounds like the very place I *should* visit," David assured her. "And, unless it's to the glory of God, I won't mention Aspidistra there, either. I'll be off and out of your way now, Mrs. F." He waved a cheery hand as he climbed into the ancient and battered green car which was more than the best he could afford.

Mrs. Featherberry watched him go and sighed again. The things he said! Well, someone had warned her about taking a redhead into her home. She hadn't listened, thinking that a ministerial probationer, no matter what the colour of his hair, would be a nice steady young man who would never put a foot out of place or say a word out of season . . . She shook her head, tolerantly, affectionately. For all his faults he had completely won her heart. She would make a little meat-pie for his lunch. She had to keep him in good trim.

David paid his one routine call, then turned Aspidistra in the direction of Crossley Road. The visiting occupied a great deal of his time, and he was endeavouring to make a survey of the entire area of the Housing Commission Estate which formed a large part of his district. Western Vale, a sprawling, sleepy outer suburb, had rested in its own green tranquillity for so many years that the invasion of the Housing Commission project had shocked and distressed it. Where the open spaces had been there sprang up row after row of small, plain homes, alike yet dissimilar, and into Western Vale there poured a cross-section of society which was almost incredible.

A new school was built, enlarged, and enlarged again. Great lengths of telephone cable were laid where cattle had peacefully grazed. The few modest, unprogressive shops lost most of their custom to the new, modern shopping centre. The old inhabitants, bewildered and resentful, sighed for the old rural peace, the days when they had known their neighbours. And the churches had come in, brimful of enthusiasm, proclaiming Western Vale as a developmental area and zealous for the planting of the seeds of the Kingdom of God in its midst. And so it was that, on this very delightful morning, the Reverend David Sterling set out to make some new contacts, and, remembering

Mrs. Featherberry's most obvious hints, to keep peace with the old, in the relatively outlying area of Crossley Road.

Mrs. McGlynn was duly visited. Mrs. Featherberry herself could have found no fault with David's deportment. He spoke of Aspidistra as "my car" and assured Mrs. McGlynn that, but for a few worthy ladies like herself, the Women's Guild would quite cease to exist. He congratulated her on the regular attendance of her children at Sunday School, on her zinnias and on her delectable home-made biscuits. He read the twenty-third Psalm and prayed with simple sincerity for Mrs. McGlynn and her household.

"And now I'll go and see the folk next-door," he said. "I think the name is Frost."

Mrs. McGlynn pursed her lips and looked as if the mere mention of such a name would bring discredit on her blameless household.

"I'm afraid you will do little good there," she said stiffly. "It pains me to live beside such a family, Mr. Sterling. And they make no effort to lift themselves. Not, of course," she added, "that one would think of *judging* them."

The Housing Commission families, according to Mrs. Featherberry, who was herself an old inhabitant of Western Vale, could be divided into two groups—those who, because of sickness or misfortune or some genuine error of judgment, had been unable to provide themselves with homes of their own, and those who had never tried. David had found this to be largely right, but there were still finer distinctions than that, and that was what made his visiting so full of surprises. It could not be said that he shook the dust of Mrs. McGlynn's establishment from his feet with either alacrity or regret, for it would be a bold speck of dust which had contrived to outwit Mrs. McGlynn's everbusy broom. Neither could it be said that he opened the Frost gate with either pleasurable anticipation or dark foreboding, for the Frost gate had long since lost its latch and was therefore never shut. He whistled as he walked up the untidy path.

The woman who answered the door might have been attractive at one time. She was a big woman, and her figure and features might have been striking had she paid some attention to them. Her hair was uncombed, a giant safety-pin did the work of two buttons on her faded, too-long dress, and she wore no shoes. She opened the door sharply, and it was clear that her hard mouth was all set for harsh speech when she caught sight of David's clerical collar and suddenly checked herself.

"I thought you were the electric light man," she said shortly.

David smiled and took a risk. There was no welcome for him here, but God opened His doors in various and unexpected ways, and it was just possible that this woman had a hidden sense of humour. He inclined his head. The boys at school had been merciless about the colour of his hair. In that moment it helped him to remember that.

"I think you could be excused for that mistake," he said with a disarming smile. "Mrs. Frost, I think?"

The woman's face relaxed.

"It's bright all right," she said almost apologetically. "I thought you'd be from the Council. They're sending someone down to-day or to-morrow to switch everything off. Unless, of course, I can pay the bill. Oh well. It won't be the first time. Or the second." She shrugged her shoulders, looking hard at David, daring him to pity or to judge. "I guess you've made a mistake. I don't go to any church."

"I was wondering," David said pleasantly, "if you have some children who might like to come to Sunday School?"

David never really knew why it was that Mrs. Frost asked him in. The house was pathetically bare and ill-furnished. A torn blind partly obscured the curtainless window of the room at the front of the house into which she took him. There was a cheap linoleum on the floor, but it bore no signs of polish or even of soap and water. There was a shoddy suite of table and stiff-backed chairs, a small unpainted cupboard piled high with comics, a half-dead fern in a yellow plastic pot on the floor, and, across one corner of the room, a large and handsome radiogram which threw into tragic relief the bitter poverty of the rest of the room.

"Andy had *that* sent home a fortnight ago," the woman said, nodding towards the corner. "He got it cheap. So cheap that it looks like we'll be paying it off for the rest of our lives." She laughed, but there was no music in the sound. "One of his mates was getting it on time-payment, and then he decided he'd get television instead, and he was looking around for someone

to take the radiogram off his hands—and of course
the first person that he saw was Andy. Andy is always
most obliging when it comes to his mates."

"Tell me about your children," David said gently,
anxious to steer his way into some subject less danger-
ous than that of the failings of Mr. Andrew Frost. "I'd
like to hear about your children."

"There's nothing to tell," she said almost sharply.
"They're no different from other people's kids. Timmy
is seven and Coral has just started school. I'm thinking
of getting a job now they're both off my hands. But
they won't be coming to Sunday School. Their father
wouldn't hear of it. He has no time for religion. Let
them decide things like that for themselves when
they're old enough, he says."

David stayed for ten minutes. More than once he
fingered the Bible in his pocket, yet some instinct told
him that he would lose the very little ground he had
gained if he opened it now. He asked permission to
pray, and the woman gave it indifferently, as if she
had let herself in for it by admitting him to the house
yet knew very well that it could make no difference
to her or to anyone else. "Dear Lord," he prayed
simply, "bless this home. Thank you for giving me
this opportunity of meeting Mrs. Frost. Amen."

"I'd like to call again," he said.

"I suppose you can if you want to," she said un-
graciously. "But I'm not coming to church. And the
kids aren't going to Sunday School."

It was as if he hadn't heard. David took out his note-
book.

"I'll make a note of the address. Number Seven Crossley Road, isn't it? Mrs. Andrew Frost."

She was almost alarmed. "Not in Andy's name," she said hastily. "It might get back to him. You never know. I'd rather you put *my* name. Mrs. Hazel Frost."

She walked to the door with him and her quick eye detected Aspidistra waiting a little distance down the road.

"Is that *your* old bomb?" she asked.

"It is," said David proudly. "Isn't she a beauty?" He glanced towards Mrs. McGlynn's. There was no-one in sight. God could use all sorts of things to win people's confidence and therefore to His glory. Even red heads. Even vintage cars. He was glad that Mrs. Featherberry was a mile away.

"Her name is Aspidistra," he said.

CHAPTER SIX

Mrs. McGlynn was planting pansies in the little bed beneath the kitchen window. She liked pansies. They were small and neat and they always kept in their place. She remembered with pardonable pride the young minister's praise of the zinnias that morning. They were particularly good this year, and some of their flaunting red and orange heads ran up to six feet and more. Mr. McGlynn had measured them.

She was not especially fond of zinnias (they were rather common, and but for Mr. McGlynn's unremitting care they would have straggled everywhere) but, growing as they did along the side fence, they served a most excellent purpose, for they formed a bright barricade between the extreme tidiness of Number Five and the disreputable contrast of Number Seven.

There was a movement on the other side of the zinnias which Mrs. McGlynn chose to disregard. She only spoke to Mrs. Frost when there was no way of getting out of it. She wondered how Mr. Sterling had got along with her. He had said some nice things at Number Five, and the best of it was that they were all true. She took another seedling and planted it an exact nine inches from its neighbour.

"I had the parson to see me this morning," said Mrs. Frost's voice through the zinnias.

Mrs. McGlynn winced. Some people had no sense

of fitness. "Mr. Sterling also called here," she said without looking up.

"He won't need to be handed out a halo when he gets to Heaven," Hazel asserted. "He'll outshine the lot with that top."

Mrs. McGlynn was shocked. Hazel could see it in the quickly-primmed mouth, the straightening of the thin shoulders. Mrs. McGlynn was not only a church member but she was also very proper. She took up another seedling and planted it but seven inches from the other.

"He wants me to send the kids to Sunday School," Hazel said hastily.

Mrs. McGlynn did not pause.

"And will you?" she asked bluntly.

"Oh, I'll have to speak to their father first," Hazel assured her. She had no intention of doing anything of the sort, but somehow she had to get the conversation on to a more agreeable level after her bad start. "I couldn't go against him in a thing like that. He has very set ideas about some things. He won't have any interference when it come to his own kids."

"He could do far worse than send them to Sunday School," said Mrs. McGlynn acidly.

There was a pause. Mrs. McGlynn continued diligently with her work. Hazel stood there, her arms folded over the safety-pin in the faded dress which she would wear until she went to bed that night. It was all right for a woman like Mrs. McGlynn to put on a clean blouse and a fresh apron at two o'clock in the afternoon. Hazel plucked one petal and then another from one of Mr. McGlynn's prized zinnias before she spoke.

"Mrs. McGlynn," she said, and there was an urgency in her voice, "did I ever tell you that I had a step-daughter?"

Mrs. McGlynn was surprised but not particularly interested. She picked up another seedling then discarded it. It would never grow. She wouldn't go to that shop again. "I didn't know that Mr. Frost had been married before," she said indifferently.

"It's nothing to do with Andy. It's only to do with me. I oughtn't to have married him—Julie's father, I mean—I wasn't his sort and he wasn't mine—but I was only nineteen, and it was wartime, and he was so lonely . . . Mrs. McGlynn, I've got to talk to someone about Julie."

Mrs. McGlynn was a prim and proper but also a practical person, and she had a kind heart. Somewhere in this jumble of words she heard the cry of an aching heart that was desperately in need of help; and she suddenly did something which, ten minutes earlier, she wouldn't have dreamed of doing.

"The rest of these seedlings are too frail to plant," she remarked, almost as if she hadn't heard a word of what Hazel had said. "Gardening is quite warm work, isn't it? I think I'd enjoy a cup of tea. Would you care to come in and have one with me?" She did not so much as glance at Hazel's bare feet. "By the time you're ready I'll have it made."

The McGlynn home, almost identical in architecture to the Frost abode, shone with polish and was dainty with flowers. The furnishings were inexpensive but in good taste, and there was a crisp yellow cloth and blue cups and saucers on the table. There were home-made biscuits, golden-brown and thick with nuts, in a little heart-shaped dish. Hazel hastily thrust her feet out of sight under the table. She told herself that she should have had the sense to put on her shoes and not her old slippers with the holes in the toes.

"You'd never think we lived next-door," she said.

Mrs. McGlynn was not to be side-tracked. She did not want Mrs. Frost to get the impression that this was anything but an occasion with a purpose. She was a firm believer in the healing power of the teapot and now, with its assistance, she must get straight to the root of the trouble and then she would know if there was anything that could be done about it. She poured the tea and passed the sugar.

"You wanted to talk about Julie, Mrs. Frost. Where does Julie live?"

"I don't know. I just don't know. That's what worries me. I sort of think I *ought* to know."

"Perhaps you'd tell me about it. From the beginning. How old was Julie when you married her father?"

"She was six. She'd be seventeen now. We never had a home. Alan was in the Air Force. They gave him compassionate leave to come home when his wife died, and they left him around Sydney after that. We just had a room—went out for meals, and that sort of thing. Alan had the money—he could afford it, and he couldn't settle. We never had Julie to live with us or even to visit us."

"She lived with her mother's people?"

"No. They had no people, either of them. Alan was

English—he lost his parents in an air raid, way back early in the war, and he didn't have any brothers or sisters. Nancy—his wife—didn't have anyone, either. I'm not sure why. I never met her. Alan never talked about her. I had enough sense not to ask him about her. It was my job to brighten him up, not to dig up his past."

"So where did Julie live?"

"In a Home. She went there when her mother died. She was only five then, and there was no-one to look after her. It was a good Home. You might even have heard of it. Roselinden."

Mrs. McGlynn nodded. Roselinden was famous, a show-place among Homes for the homeless. "And did you ever visit her there?"

"Oh yes. Every visiting-day. The first Saturday in every month. Alan wangled leave most of the times. Sometimes I went alone." She paused and took more sugar with her own spoon instead of the one provided by Mrs. McGlynn. "It was easier then," she went on reflectively. "They were both so quiet, Alan and Julie. I had to do all the talking for three." She laughed. "You wouldn't think that was any hardship, I guess. But they couldn't seem to find one another, if you get what I mean. As if they were frightened of one another, or something. It was the place itself that frightened *me*. It was all so big, and fancy, and thick with rules as these biscuits are with nuts. You never knew if you were putting your left foot where your right one ought to be."

"And Julie's father? Was he——"

"We were only married nine months when it

happened. It was a crash, of course. It upset me a lot. Alan was a good few years older than I was, as you'll have guessed. It was only a couple of days after I was twenty. Julie was seven."

Mrs. McGlynn looked across the table at her visitor. Everything about Hazel was slipshod—the cheaply-waved hair, the smear of lipstick misapplied, the gap where the tooth should have been, the faded dress with the buttons missing. And she knew all about the slippers with both toes out. Yet—she could have been a pretty girl.

"You poor soul," she said. "Have another cup of tea."

Hazel shook her head. "I shouldn't have married him. I told you that out by the fence. He was too good for me. You could see he'd come from a good family. I couldn't keep up with him and I guess it was all for the best that he was taken. I couldn't have made him happy, not once the war was over and he had to live with me every day."

"And did you keep going to see Julie?"

"I never missed. Not until I got engaged to Andy. That was two years later. He said we'd have enough troubles of our own without taking on other people's and that Julie would be better off if she stayed where she was. He was right enough in *that*. I just couldn't see Alan's kid in *there* with us." She gave a bitter little laugh. "No-one could say that I married above myself *twice*!"

"And you didn't see Julie again?" asked Mrs. McGlynn, feeling that it was safer and more diplomatic to dwell on the past rather than the present. It was beyond all the bounds of neighbourliness that she should criticise Mr. Frost to his own wife, poor though her opinion of him might be. "At Christmas, maybe. Or on her birthday?"

"Andy put his foot down. He said it had to be Julie or him. He was jealous. That was all. I should have stood up to him. I know that now. Eight years I've had Julie on my conscience but I—well, it was easier to do nothing about it. Andy can be awkward if he's crossed. I just left the people at the Home to explain to Julie."

"And you've no idea where she is now?"

"Not the slightest. She'd leave the Home when she was fifteen. That was one of their brass-bound rules. I remember that."

Mrs. McGlynn hesitated. She didn't know much about Homes like Roselinden, but she presumed that they would continue to exercise guardianship over orphan wards until they were of age. It was therefore quite probable that a simple enquiry might quickly reveal Julie's whereabouts. It all depended on how badly Mrs. Frost wanted to find her . . .

"Do you really want to know where she is?" asked Mrs. McGlynn bluntly. "Has something particularly stirred your conscience to-day, Mrs. Frost?"

It was a straight question but a fair one. Hazel acknowledged that. She flushed.

"It was the young fellow," she said almost apologetically. "The young fellow with the red hair. Mrs. McGlynn, I'm sorry I said that about him before. I liked him. I've never had a parson in my house before and

I don't mind telling you that I've never wanted one. Maybe there is a God and maybe there isn't. I can only say that, if there is, He's never bothered Himself about *me*. It wasn't that the young fellow said anything in particular—it was just that he was in my house and I knew that I had this on my mind—and he says that he'll be coming back again and I know that I've got to do something quickly. . . ."

"It would only take you an hour or so to get to Roselinden," said Mrs. McGlynn firmly. She had found the trouble. She must administer the medicine and then her visitor could go. "They will almost certainly be able to give you some information or at least make some enquiries for you. You must go as soon as possible. Go to-morrow."

In her mind's eye Hazel saw Roselinden, stately, immense, perfectly organised. No, she couldn't do it. Not even for Julie. Not even for the parson boy with the red hair. It had been awesome enough when she'd had pretty clothes and clever make-up, very high heels and youthful confidence. No, she couldn't do it. That haughty woman might still be there in the office. She'd looked too pleased with herself to be the marrying kind. To face Roselinden was just not possible. There must be some other way. She thought quickly.

"I think it would be better to write," she said. "It might be a week or so before I can spare the time to go in person. I guess I'd better get along, Mrs. McGlynn. The kids will be in from school before I know where I am. Thanks for asking me in. It's done me good to talk. And those biscuits are real nice."

"I could give you the recipe if you like," said Mrs. McGlynn.

It was a magnanimous offer, a noble offer. Mrs. McGlynn was known to be very close with her recipes. But Hazel, even in her softened frame of mind, would go so far but no farther. She didn't bother to bake nowadays. It was too big an effort. And in any case the man from the Council was sure to be down to cut off the electricity—that was a good excuse. She'd try to slip in half-a-pound of biscuits on her next grocery order, though she was already three weeks behind in her payment and the grocer was beginning to get an all-too-familiar look in his eye when she went beyond the essentials of sugar and butter and tea. . . .

She shook her head. "There's something wrong with my oven," she said glibly. "I'm expecting the Council man to see about it any day. No, thanks, Mrs. McGlynn. Andy would really rather have the bought ones."

CHAPTER SEVEN

MISS BLAKE carried the letter to Julie in person. On second thoughts Hazel had decided to write to Julie herself. That took less effort than addressing the dignified Roselinden authorities, for Hazel was no scholar and the composition of even the simplest letter taxed her resources greatly. It was no trouble to explain her change of tactics to Mrs. McGlynn.

"If they know where she is they'll re-address it," she reasoned logically. "If they don't they'll send it back."

They did not need to send it back. Neither did they re-address it. On the afternoon of its arrival Miss Blake set out to walk the pleasant tree-lined mile between Roselinden and the Loch residence. It was Miss Blake's afternoon off, and the thought of seeing Julie again was a pleasurable one. She had missed Julie more than she would care to say, and Daffodil Baker, who had taken over Julie's duties, was the poorest hand at everything and was straining Miss Blake's patience to the limit. It would be good to air her grievances to Julie.

She had had no opportunity of seeing Julie in the five weeks since her departure from Cottage Two. Everything had gone wrong that could go wrong. Miss Blake herself had had influenza, the painters had been in downstairs, the cook had left almost without warning and it had taken Miss Levering ten days to find someone to take her place. Miss Blake had found herself almost entirely tied to the house. Miss Levering had called on Julie on two occasions and had taken back a very pleasing report, but that wasn't the same as hearing it from Julie herself. Miss Blake quickened her steps as the lovely old Loch home came into sight.

With her finger on the doorbell Miss Blake paused.

Inside the house someone was singing, and the tune was the tune of a hymn. Miss Blake had come from a good church-going family, and she recognised a hymn tune when she heard it even on a Tuesday afternoon. She couldn't fit any words to it, but verse after verse the singer sang, to a soft pianoforte accompaniment, and somehow Miss Blake couldn't bring herself to push the doorbell until the last notes trailed away in a silver ripple of arpeggios. Then she rang.

Julie, ironing her frocks in the little room appointed for such duties, had missed not one word. Mrs. Loch was out, and only Marguerite and Julie were at home. This was unusual. Mrs. Loch mostly contrived to take Marguerite with her. Julie understood. Mrs. Loch had made it very plain. But to-day Marguerite was at home, although Mrs. Loch had not left her without occupation. She had given her daughter a bundle of circulars, a pile of envelopes, and a long list of names. Marguerite knew what must be done with them, and she had promised her mother that it should be done.

Her voice was untrained but appealingly sweet and true. Marguerite's voice, and Marguerite's face, had stirred more than one church congregation. Music came to her almost as naturally as breathing, and she lost all sense of time and responsibility when she was seated at the piano. Mrs. Loch's circulars were entirely forgotten. Marguerite was in a world of her own, borne thither by the hushed and simple melody of the tune 'Beatitudo' and the soul-words of a man who had lived two centuries earlier:

> *O Jesus Christ, grow Thou in me,*
> *And all things else recede:*
> *My heart be daily nearer Thee*
> *From sin be daily freed.*
>
> *Fill me with gladness from above,*
> *Hold me by strength divine!*
> *Lord, let the glow of Thy great love*
> *Through my whole being shine.*
>
> *Make this poor self grow less and less,*
> *Be Thou my life and aim;*
> *O make me daily, through Thy grace,*
> *More meet to bear Thy name!*

Julie, listening, believed that those words might have been especially written for Marguerite. Roselinden training had been of the highest moral standard. Religion had been taught from its earliest beginnings. Old Mr. Rose had seen to that, and Miss Levering had enforced his instructions to the letter. Evening prayers, Sunday morning service in the lovely little chapel, Sunday School classes taught by visiting teachers, a Bible in the possession of each girl—Miss Levering permitted no latitude whatsoever regarding any of these.

Roselinden acknowledged God. It revered Him. Had He not provided for old Mr. Rose and his wife and those first two little girls when no-one else had cared what happened to them? But He was made to seem a distant, impersonal God. Even the Sunday School teachers, although they had tried very hard, had never succeeded in making God seem close and real and approachable. Roselinden had set Him on too remote a pedestal for any outsider to bring Him nearer to those within its very walls. Mrs. Loch, thought Julie, must have the same sort of God . . . .

But Marguerite's God was different. To Marguerite, as to old Mr. Rose, God was real, God was known as a very dear, very faithful friend is known. Julie sighed a little as she pressed a straight pleat into one of the pastel cottons which Miss Levering had chosen. It would be nice to be like Marguerite, but it was quite, quite impossible. God could be seen in Marguerite because He *was* in her. That was all there was about it. It was puzzling, it was beyond understanding, but it was true.

The sound of the doorbell eased the tension of her thoughts. She hoped that the caller had heard Marguerite singing. She went on with her ironing. Mrs. Loch (who was determined to be strictly just in her relationships with Julie) had decreed that, unless alone in the house, Julie was not to be expected to answer the door between the hours of two and four. Those hours were to be Julie's own.

The doorbell always represented the unknown and

possibly interesting to Marguerite. One could never tell who might be there or what their mission might be. Momentarily her thoughts flicked to Julie. Julie could be depended upon to produce a cup of tea on a dainty tray if needed. She opened the door with a certain measure of pleasant anticipation.

Let it not be thought that the sight of plain, respectable Miss Blake on the doorstep was in any way dashing to Marguerite. On the other hand, Miss Blake's polite "Good afternoon. Could I speak to Julie Westaway, please?" opened up, in Marguerite's lively imagination, the most intriguing possibilities. She did not, at first, recognise Miss Blake. She had seen her only on the day of Julie's arrival, and then she had been in her grey Roselinden uniform with a stiff white hat. For one moment Marguerite believed that her prayers had been answered. This strange person in a brown skirt and blue cardigan was someone belonging to Julie. Her heart sang. She had prayed for this very thing. Then she recognised Miss Blake, and her face fell.

"I thought you were one of Julie's long-lost relatives," she said. "Do come in, Miss Blake. Julie will be so pleased to see you."

"If I was one of Julie's relatives I wouldn't be long-lost," Miss Blake said significantly. She had seen that sort of thing happen too often—people neglecting a poor child, shamefully, for all the years that she was at Roselinden, and then turning up, without apology, without any feeling, as soon as the girl was old enough to leave school and earn some money. Better that Julie should have no-one than someone like *that*.

"I'll call Julie." Miss Blake looked so very respect-able that Marguerite felt that she should be showing her into Mrs. Loch's sitting-room, but her mother had specified the sun-room for Julie's callers, so the sun-room it had better be. "Julie doesn't have many visitors. I'm so glad that you came, Miss Blake."

There was such pleasure in Julie's face when she came that Miss Blake, who had never had, never would have, a daughter of her own, suddenly realised how much of her affection had been centred upon Julie Westaway. But she held out her hand stiffly, formally. It was not easy for Miss Blake to be demonstrative.

"If you'd like to let me know when there's a cup of tea about I could come and have it with you," Marguerite suggested. Her disappointment had van-ished. God might not answer her prayers quickly, but He would answer them. "I have a job to do now for Mummy."

She went off, singing. The words floated back.

Lord, let the glow of Thy great love
Through my whole being shine.

A moment later the notes of 'My Jesus, I love Thee' came softly from the piano.

"She's lovely," Julie breathed.

"She's different from what I expected," Miss Blake conceded. She added, a little acidly, "Didn't she say she had a job to do for her mother?"

"Oh, I'll help her with *that*," Julie assured her, although she hadn't the faintest idea of what the job might be. "I haven't much to do. Just the vegetables, at half-past four. I could do the beans as we talk, couldn't I? Oh, it *is* nice to see you, Miss Blake. I want to hear about everything. Miss Levering said she thought Daffodil Baker would be taking over my work."

Miss Blake paused in the act of opening her handbag. She had been just about to give the letter to Julie. But that could wait. It wasn't likely to be urgent. The subject of Daffodil Baker's shortcomings could be thrashed out first.

Miss Blake put her handbag on the floor beside her chair. "Bring two knives, Julie," she said. "I'll help you with the beans. As for Daffodil Baker . . ."

At three o'clock Julie made a cup of tea.

Mrs. Loch would have considered it a most incorrect hour for afternoon tea, but that was when the matrons at Roselinden always had it, before the girls came in from school. Julie wanted Miss Blake to feel at home. Making people feel at home would be Julie's speciality always.

Conversationally much ground had been covered. Neither Miss Blake nor Julie would, in ordinary circumstances, have been accused of being talkative; but this was an occasion on which both had much to say. They went from Daffodil Baker to Miss Terry, the new cook; from Miss Terry to Miss Levering, from Miss Levering back to Daffodil Baker. Julie enquired about Lexie, about Adrienne. Adrienne was still at Roselinden, temporarily, while her grandmother was in hospital. Lexie had come back with Alice, to pick up something or the other—Miss Blake couldn't remember what. There was a new bread-slicer in the kitchen, put there by the directors, and the ladies' committee was thinking about replacing all the linen bedspreads with chenille ones so that there wouldn't be so much ironing. . . .

"You're very comfortable here, Julie," Miss Blake said. She looked around the pleasant sun-room with its gay curtains and casual furnishings. She dropped her voice. The music had ceased. "Are you happy, Julie?"

"I like the work," Julie said, as if weighing each word before entrusting it to even Miss Blake's hearing. "I like beautiful things. Good things. They're all like that here. I like keeping things beautiful, Miss Blake. I—there just isn't any other kind of work that I *could* do."

"And Mrs. Loch?" Miss Blake prompted her, whispering.

"She is very kind. It isn't hard, Miss Blake. I try not to make mistakes."

"Mr. Loch?" The whisper dropped lower.

"I don't really see him much. He never asks me to do anything for him. I—I wouldn't know how to talk to him."

"And Miss Loch?"

"She's lovely," Julie repeated. "Miss Blake, I'd do anything, *anything*, for her. She isn't like other people. She *shines*, somehow." It was, Julie knew, a most inadequate description—but how could one put into words the light that was Marguerite? "You won't mind, will you, if she comes to have afternoon tea with us?"

At ten minutes to four Miss Blake said good-bye. She
had learned a number of things. Julie was a fortunate,
a most fortunate, girl. She was apparently giving satisfaction, which spoke well for Roselinden training.
Clearly she stood in much awe of Mrs. Loch, but that
was only to be expected. The girl Marguerite was a
little difficult to understand. She was friendly, most
friendly, and what Julie had said was true enough—
she did *shine*, in a way that you couldn't explain. She
was quite different from her mother, quite different
from what Miss Blake had expected, yet in some way
which was quite beyond explaining, Miss Blake had
the curious feeling that all the time she was being put
through an examination. . . .

"Well, that was nice," said Marguerite, as the door
closed behind the visitor. "I like meeting new people
and finding out all about them. It's all good deaconess
practice. And now, Julie, are you terribly busy? It's
just occurred to me that Mummy gave me a little job
to do. Invitations or something. They have to be folded
and put into envelopes."

But the circulars were destined to remain unfolded
until the next day when Mrs. Loch, her mouth pressed
coldly into a thin line of displeasure, did them for herself. The doorbell rang sharply. Miss Blake was on the
doorstep again.

"I must apologise," she said stiffly. "I have a letter
for Julie."

CHAPTER EIGHT

The letter was brief. Hazel wasted no words when it came to pen and ink.

> 7 Crossley Road,
> Western Vale.
> March 5.

Dear Julie,

I suppose you've just about forgotten me. I've been thinking about you and suppose you're in a job now. I'm sorry I didn't go back to see you at the Home. You may not believe this, but it was someone else's fault. Still, I should have gone, for your father's sake. He was too good for me, as I suppose even a kid like you could have seen. I would like to know where you are now. That is, if you ever get this.

> Yours truly,
> Hazel.

P.S. My name is now Mrs. Frost.

"It's from my stepmother," Julie said without expression. She handed the letter to Marguerite. Had Marguerite looked at the girl instead of the letter she would have seen that her face was masked with white.

The radiance came into Marguerite's eyes as she read the ill-written sentences. She hadn't been so far wrong after all. Miss Blake *had* come in answer to her prayers. The fact that the letter wasn't very well-constructed didn't mean a thing.

"I knew that there must be someone somewhere," she said softly.

The resentment which had for eight years been pent-up in Julie's heart suddenly spilled over. Julie, with long years of Roselinden experience behind her, knew almost as much as Miss Blake about the kind of relatives who kept right out of sight until a pay envelope came into view. That Hazel's motive could possibly be a sincere one did not so much as occur to her.

"There *isn't* anyone," she said passionately. "I never want to see—*her*—again. She could have come some-times. She knew I had no-one else. I don't need her now. She's found out something from someone. She's found out that I'm in a good home, with good money . . . I remember when Dorrie Brooke's grand-father came to get her. She was fifteen, and he hadn't been to see her *once*."

The girl shuddered at the remembrance of the dread-ful old man, the toothless younger woman who was Dorrie's aunt. "And she had to go with them," she said, her voice quivering. "They proved their relation-ship and she had to go." She sat down suddenly and burst into tears.

Marguerite hesitated. This wasn't like Julie. As a deaconess she would undoubtedly have to handle all sorts of awkward situations, but she was still only a deaconess-to-be and she simply did not know what to do with this one. She grasped at the straw which was, in reality, a solid plank.

"I don't think that could happen to you, Julie," she said, and she hoped that she spoke with the voice of assurance. "Your stepmother isn't exactly related to you, is she? And—it seems an honest letter, Julie. She says she's sorry about it all."

"I never want to see her again," Julie repeated, the words so drenched in sobs that they were almost drowned. "She—she didn't come when I needed her. Someone's been talking to her. . . ."

"Perhaps it was God," Marguerite said simply.

There was something in the quiet words that checked Julie's tears. She did not in the least agree with Marguerite. That God should be concerned about her affairs at all was beyond the bounds of probability; that He could do nothing better than bring the unfaithful Hazel back into her life was equally unlikely. But to say these things would be hurtful to Marguerite, and because of that she must not say them. She wiped her eyes.

"I'm sorry," she quavered. She did not say for what, and something restrained Marguerite from enquiring. She turned her attention back to the letter itself. "I don't even know where Western Vale is," she said.

"Daddy will know," Marguerite assured her, glad to have something practical to offer. "It's probably one of the newer suburbs. I expect your—Mrs. Frost thought that you would know."

"I never thought of her as being different from my father," Julie said slowly. "She *was* different, of course. She talked a lot, and laughed—but he was always so quiet. It's not very easy to remember much about him," she confessed. "I was only seven when he died. It's much easier to remember Hazel. She was only young—Miss Levering said she was just nineteen when she married my father . . . And I'm seventeen, Marguerite. It's hard to piece it all together now." She sighed forlornly, but all the tears were gone, and she was quiet, reserved Julie Westaway again. "It isn't a very good letter, is it? I expect what she says is right. She wasn't the same sort of person as my father, but I never knew."

"You don't remember your own mother, do you, Julie?"

"Not very well. She must have been sick most of the time. I can't remember her doing things for me. It's all very vague, as if there's a shadow over those years. The thing I remember most is her voice. She spoke so softly. Perhaps that was because she was sick." A swift flash of enlightenment came to Julie. "I remember now. Hazel never spoke softly. I sometimes used to wish that she would."

She sighed again. "I wish Miss Blake had remembered the letter earlier. She knew all about Hazel. She could have told me what to do."

Marguerite told the story, with some pardonable dramatic touches, immediately after dinner that evening. With Julie's permission she showed Hazel's letter to her parents. Julie, conscientiously washing the dishes in the kitchen, would have given her ears to hear what was being said, yet she had never felt more glad to be out of a discussion.

Mr. Loch cut straight to the core of the matter.

"Julie is legally a ward of Roselinden," he assured the anxious Marguerite. "Nothing can alter that. This woman has no legal claim on her whatsoever and Julie need have no fear that she will successfully bring any pressure to bear." He turned to the letter again.

"I agree with you, Daisybud," he said. "There is a ring of sincerity about this. Something has stirred the woman's conscience."

"Or Some*one*," Marguerite corrected him softly. She did not usually find it easy to speak to her father about the things that were nearest to her heart, but the old childish endearment seemed to bring him closer to her understanding.

He smiled at her but did not continue the line of thought. "It isn't the letter of an educated person. She is possibly in poor circumstances, yet I do not feel that she is asking anything more than some measure of reconciliation with Julie. I see no reason why Julie should not go to see her."

"Do you know where Western Vale is, Daddy?"

"I know the general locality. One of our men lives even further up the line. It wouldn't be more than an hour's run by train from here. It's one of those places that used to be rural but has suddenly (and regrettably, I think) become closely settled. This Mrs. Frost probably lives in a Housing Commission home."

"OH!" The lamp lit itself in Marguerite's eyes. To such places a deaconess was sometimes appointed. She must see it. She must meet Mrs. Frost. It would be such excellent experience. She clasped her hands and looked longingly at her mother.

"Julie isn't used to travelling alone," she said. "She could so easily make a mistake about the train or something. Don't you think it would be wise for me to go with her, Mummy?"

"I most certainly do not," Mrs. Loch said sharply. The conversation had been of small interest to her. It was clear that this connection of Julie's was a person of little importance. "Julie is seventeen and she must learn to be responsible for herself. She can go on her day off as soon as she likes, but it is better *in every way* that she should go alone."

"But, Mummy——"

"That is my answer, Marguerite."

"I think that Marguerite is right," Mr. Loch said unexpectedly. "We must remember that *we* are responsible for Julie, Gwen. If Julie wishes to visit this woman (I would not press it, my dear, but with a little encouragement I think that she *will* go) I do not think that she should go alone."

"You may be right," said Mrs. Loch, her stiffly-starched tone implying that she very much doubted it. "But it will be necessary for Julie to change her day off. Mrs. Stacey would be most disappointed if Marguerite missed her Wednesday's tennis."

On the Thursday of the following week the two girls set out for Western Vale. Julie had needed more than a little persuasion. The passionate resentment against Hazel had quietened, but in its place there was a hard indifference which Marguerite found even more difficult to understand. Julie had refused to go without

Miss Levering's approval, so entirely bound up with Roselinden was every thought of Hazel, but Mrs. Loch had speedily settled that over the telephone. While little good could be expected from such a visit, Miss Levering said, there was an equal probability of little harm, for Julie enjoyed the protection of not only Roselinden but of Mr. and Mrs. Philip Loch; and this Mrs. Frost (Miss Levering unbent sufficiently to pass her own judgment on Mrs. Frost to Mrs. Loch) would find that any hopes of gain through her first husband's daughter were disappointingly groundless. Julie should visit her—once. There would then be no need for any further association.

Marguerite's conviction that God's hand was in it all somewhere did not convince Julie in the least. She was finding it very difficult to become acquainted with God. She read her Bible and her Scripture Union notes faithfully, for the almost sole purpose of pleasing Marguerite, but there was still so much that she did not understand. It was the same when she went to church on Sunday nights with Marguerite. The old minister at Deveringham Road put it all so simply, but Julie felt that she was like a child who had come into a school class halfway through the year and had missed so many of the lessons that it was impossible to catch up . . . .

"How shall I introduce you?" Julie asked nervously, as they found their way from Western Vale station to Crossley Road. She was wishing within herself that they had not come but it would never do for

Marguerite to know that. It was Marguerite who had enthusiasm in her step.

"This is my friend, Marguerite Loch." Marguerite smiled at Julie with the encouragement of real affection. "I *am* your friend, you know, Julie."

"Thank you," said Julie humbly. To her they seemed more like princess and lady-in-waiting than two friends. She looked covertly at Marguerite. How lovely she was, with the early autumn sunshine highlighting the gold in her hair and her face illumined by some nameless inner glory! It did not occur to Julie that those who passed by saw two pretty girls and not Marguerite only. She did not realise that a delicate refinement of face and form, emphasised by a naturally shy and sweet demeanour, gave to her a charm which, to some eyes, might seem of greater beauty than Marguerite's more striking loveliness.

"You always introduce the younger person to the older," Marguerite continued. "I wonder what Mrs. Frost will be like. Julie, I'm so glad we've come."

It had to be admitted. "I'm not," said Julie flatly.

The walk to Crossley Road was long and dusty and monotonous. They passed house after house, small and unpretentious, one with red gates and letter-box, one with yellow or green, one with a garden and gay, trim windowboxes and the next with grass knee-high. Marguerite was fascinated. In such a community a deaconess would be a person of prestige. No such thoughts came to Julie. She was simply and desperately hoping that Hazel would live in one of the tidier houses.

They turned at last into Crossley Road. Here there were houses on one side of the road only. On the other was a pleasant little farm, not yet swept away by the broom of closer settlement in the name of progress. Beyond the farm stood the hills, tree-clad and green.

Marguerite spoke softly.

"I'm glad there are trees," she said.

"It's Number Seven," Julie whispered nervously. "One—three—I hope Hazel got my letter."

She looked without hope at Mrs. McGlynn's spotless front steps, at the brave brightness of the sentinel zinnias. Number Five. It couldn't be otherwise, of course. Number Seven must be the poverty-marked little place next door. . . .

There was a battered and antiquated green car in the street outside. Julie paid little attention to it. She followed Marguerite through the ever-open gateway and unwillingly lifted her eyes to the small front verandah. There, talking to a woman who could be none other than Hazel, was a young man with a clerical collar and the reddest of red hair.

Julie, walking up the overgrown path a pace or two behind the eager crusader tread of Marguerite, was conscious of one thing only, and that was a swift, selfless compassion. She could feel no resentment towards a Hazel who lived and looked like *this*. But nothing of her inner pity showed in her set young face. Hazel, coming forward to meet her, told herself that she would have known Julie anywhere. She had her father's erect carriage, his reserve, his pride. To Hazel, in that moment, Julie was Alan Westaway personified, and all the old sense of inferiority, the old lack of confidence which she associated with both Alan and Roselinden, took possession of her.

She put out her hand, awkwardly, scarcely expecting that Julie would take it. In the old days she had kissed Julie, kissed her often and with real affection because she was sincerely fond of her. It was quite unthinkable that this girl with Alan's aloofness should be kissed.

"Julie," she said slowly. She could think of no other word to say.

Julie's good Roselinden training came to her aid. She shook hands with dignity. "How do you do, Hazel?" she said formally. She added, obediently: "This is my friend, Marguerite Loch."

David Sterling stepped forward. "You have visitors, Mrs. Frost. I'll come back some other time."

"This is Mr. Reverend Sterling." For the moment Hazel had completely forgotten him. "And this is my— my——" she baulked, unable to openly identify this girl of Alan's as her stepdaughter—"this is Miss Julie Westaway." She looked at Marguerite and apologised nervously. "I'm afraid I didn't catch your name."

Marguerite held out her hand with the curious certainty that she needed no introduction. God's hand was in *this*, surely. It was as if she and David Sterling had known one another always. She read it in his eyes as clearly as he must read it in hers.

"I am Marguerite Loch," she said.

CHAPTER NINE

THE visit was, surprisingly, a success.

Marguerite, delighted with the promising manner of its beginning, was at her brightest and most charming. Within five minutes she had won Hazel's confidence, and within ten they were Hazel and Marguerite to one another. Julie's reserve thawed slowly as her compassion deepened and as she began to see the old, vivid Hazel through this stranger who was Mrs. Frost. Yet she could find no words in which to express herself. It was Marguerite who did all the talking.

Julie had never before been in a home that was not thoroughly respectable. Roselinden and Mrs. Loch, of course, maintained extraordinarily high standards; but Miss Blake's relatives, the Sunday School teachers, and Lexie's cousin Alice all lived in surroundings of cleanliness and thrift. She had not imagined that anyone *could* live as Hazel and her family apparently did live. Yet Hazel had made, for her, a very real effort.

She had endeavoured to mend the torn blind (thereby making matters worse than they had been before) and she had moved the chairs and even the table when she swept the floor. She had almost gone so far as to remove the fern in the yellow plastic pot from the floor, for it was three-quarters dead and spasmodic watering seemed no longer of any avail; but she thought better of that. There were no flowers in the room, for there were none nearer than Mrs. McGlynn's; but, from the recesses of the kitchen cupboard, Hazel had brought to light a large green china frog and she had perched it, without dusting, on top of the now higher pile of comics on the unpainted cupboard. She had even prepared an afternoon tea of sorts, for Julie's brief, curt little note had mentioned that she would be bringing a friend.

The grocer had proved lenient, to the extent of half-a-pound of extremely plain biscuits, and she had borrowed sufficient from the money long-promised to the butcher to buy a square of chocolate cake and two bottles of lemonade. She felt a bit badly about the lemonade, but the Council had finally made good its threat and had cut off the electricity supply, pending payment of Mr. Frost's account, so a cup of tea was out of the question. And what had it mattered, she'd asked herself, as she made her few preparations? What did anything matter? Life was much simpler, less perplexing, when you took the easy way in everything. Yet—was it? Hazel, looking at Julie, wondered how she could possibly hope to bridge the gulf of eight years.

She looked less like Alan as Hazel became accustomed to her. She had his bearing, his quiet pride, but neither his colouring nor his features. She was close enough to being pretty, Hazel thought; but it was Marguerite, friendly, glowing Marguerite, who had won Hazel's heart. . . .

At half-past three Timmy and Coral came in from school, both so grubby, so thin, and so noticeably un-patched that Marguerite was enchanted. She had always had a passionate desire to do something worth-while for the under-privileged, but few such children had ever crossed her path and certainly none had been so blatantly under-privileged as Timmy and Coral Frost. She bore them off with her, not altogether will-ingly, to the little neglected backyard which could have been a flourishing garden had Mr. Andrew Frost seen fit to turn the sod and sow the seed.

"Let's play something," she suggested. Julie and Hazel were getting just nowhere. A few minutes on their own was what they needed. "Have you a ball, Timmy?"

Within the house the conversation at first came slowly, haltingly. Hazel rested her elbows on the table and cupped her thickening chin in her hands. "You're lucky," she said awkwardly. "Getting a job with *her* mother."

"Yes," said Julie. Marguerite would have said that it wasn't a matter of luck. "Yes, I am."

There was a pause. "I suppose she's very particular."

"Yes. Very."

"How long did you say you'd been there?"

"Seven weeks."

"I suppose that woman is still in the office at the Home."

"Miss Levering? Oh, yes. Miss Blake is still at Cot-tage Two," Julie added, grateful for some thought which could be put into words.

"I didn't like that woman in the office," Hazel said suddenly. "She knew too much. I might have put it over you, Julie, but I never put it over *her*. She saw clean through me, and I knew it." She looked straight into Julie's eyes, trying to read something there. "And I wasn't like *this*—then."

"I know," said Julie. She wished immediately that she hadn't said it. It wasn't tactful. It gave acknowledgment to the fact that Hazel had let herself slip. "I shouldn't have said that," she apologised.

"You were only speaking the truth," the woman said without bitterness. Suddenly, timidly, she put out a hand and patted Julie's. "I don't mind what you say, kid, so long as you say something. You're too much like your father, just sitting there, not letting me know what you think. Yet—Julie, I honestly believe that he was fond of me."

"So was I," said Julie loyally. She had no possible doubt of her own affection for the old Hazel. The admission somehow eased the tightness within her and made possible a question which was the one vital question. "Hazel, did you know my mother at all?"

Hazel shook her head. "I never met her. I wouldn't have met your dad if I hadn't been helping in the canteen where he was stationed. I felt sorry for him. I was only nineteen—two years older than you are now, Julie—he was quite a bit older, of course. I used to talk to him, and then he began to take me out, and within three months we were married. People did things like that during the war. He never took me among his own friends. It was as if he wanted to make a fresh start, so that he could forget. He only took me to see *you*."

Hazel hesitated. "I was sorry for you, too, Julie. In a different way, of course. You were so much like him. You sort of built a shell around yourself and the people who liked you had to like the shell, too. Alan was like that. You make things hard for yourself." She dropped her eyes, unable to meet Julie's as she went on. "I suppose you've never forgiven me for what I did, but you can see it was all for the best, can't you? I never had a home that was good enough for *you*, even if they'd let you come to live with me, which they wouldn't have. I married Andy in a housing shortage and we went to live in what you'd call the slums. We only left because they were going to pull down the house before it fell down. And then——" she laughed ironically—"we came *here*."

"You must have been glad," Julie ventured. She had seen the sort of dwelling in which Hazel must have lived. Miss Blake had pointed out the backs of rows and rows of such places, soot-begrimed, on one occasion when she had taken Julie into Sydney by train. Now, beneath the torn edges of the blind, she could see the clean green of hills, the sweep of willows around the curve of the creek, the neat farm-buildings, white-painted.

"I hate it," the woman said vehemently. "There we were all of a kind. It's different here. I look at the woman next-door and I see how far I've let myself go and I don't care *that* much." She snapped her fingers scornfully at the possible opinion of good Mrs. McGlynn. "And then——" was there a suspicion of a tear in Hazel's hard eye? "——the parson boy comes and I know I *should* care."

"He seems very young," Julie said timidly. The clergymen who had visited Roselinden had all seemed elderly, and old Mr. Cartwright at Deveringham Road had white hair.

"Oh, he's only a learner—says he should have the L on himself, seeing that he doesn't need it on his old bomb. I like him," Hazel said confidentially. "He's got something about him. Something the same as your friend Marguerite. I can't explain what."

"I think I know what you mean," Julie said slowly. It was what old Mr. Rose must have had, too. "I can't explain it either, Hazel."

At four o'clock Marguerite took over the situation again. The game with the under-privileged Timmy and Coral had proved a somewhat energetic one, and she felt a little warm and dishevelled but otherwise well pleased with the whole afternoon.

"We've quite a walk ahead of us, Julie," she said. "And you'll want to get on with cooking your dinner, I expect, Hazel."

"There's no hurry," said Hazel with perfect truthfulness. It wasn't going to take long to put a loaf of bread and a tin of jam, a jar of peanut butter and the remains of the chocolate cake on the table. It was bad to be out of favour with the grocer and the butcher *and* the Council all at once, and Thursday was always the leanest day of the week, with Andy not being paid until Friday. "There's no hurry," she repeated. "Andy may be late."

"We must come again," Marguerite assured her. "It's been a really lovely afternoon, Hazel. I've always liked meeting new people. I'm going to be a deaconess, you know."

"There's a train at twenty-five past four. You'll get it easy if you step it out," said Hazel practically. Marguerite must be getting mixed up somewhere. Deaconesses were the sort of people you tried to dodge unless you knew for certain that they were handing out something. "Yes, come again. It's done me good, seeing you both."

Julie lingered for one moment at the top of the unwashed steps. Marguerite, with the admiring Timmy on one side and Coral on the other, was already halfway down the path. Julie looked at Hazel. Life turned things upside down in so many ways. It was now Julie who was the visitor, Hazel the visited, Julie the stronger, Hazel the needier. With a pity mingled with an old-rooted affection she turned and kissed the woman on the roughened cheek.

"I'll come back," she said.

It wasn't altogether easy to obey Hazel's injunction to "step it out." The road to the station was roundabout and uneven, and Marguerite, who had expended considerable energy on the game in the Frost backyard, found her feet dragging rebelliously before they had covered half of the distance; and Julie, who had worn her new high-heeled shoes to give her confidence, was wishing that she hadn't. Marguerite had never been more

sure of God's provision for her temporal needs than
she was when an ancient and dilapidated green car
rattled to a standstill two yards ahead of them. *This*
was no coincidence.

"You have saved my feet from chronic disablement
and Julie's heels from immediate destruction," Marguerite said gaily. "This is the very nicest thing that could
have happened, Mr. Sterling. Isn't it, Julie?"

"Yes," said Julie briefly. She knew that any words
of hers would fall so short of Marguerite's in wit and
brilliance that they would be quite unnoticed. She
scrambled gratefully after Marguerite into the front
seat of the car.

"I think that, too," said David, sliding into his seat
beside Marguerite and including Julie in the orbit of
his smile. "Aspidistra and I feel most honoured, as a
matter of fact."

Marguerite was delighted. She laughed appreciatively at the nonsense which she instantly understood.
Julie was glad that there was no need for her to speak.
It was as though the others had known one another
from the beginning of time. In no time at all they made
it plain that they liked the same things, they spoke
the same language, they even knew some of the
same people. Old Mr. Cartwright at Deveringham
Road was one of David's oldest friends. He had been
minister of the very church where David had grown
up. Marguerite was thrilled. She loved Mr. Cartwright.
She told David about her singing, and he told her
that it would be just wonderful if she could come
and sing at one of his services at Western Vale

some Sunday evening . . . It was all just as simple as that.

They reached the station seven minutes ahead of the train. David walked on to the platform with them. The conversation flowed around Julie, touching her only occasionally with its furthermost ripples. She was glad to see the automatic railway gates swing down, indicating that the train was due.

She shook hands with David shyly, remembering her Roselinden manners where the clergy was concerned.

"I'm pleased to have met you," she murmured.

CHAPTER TEN

JULIE was knitting. It was a pastime which she had always enjoyed but at which, unlike Lexie, she had never excelled. At the end of her first week with Mrs. Loch she had purchased needles and blue wool and a simple pattern and had made a painstaking beginning with a jumper for herself. Now, on the Saturday of the week following her visit to Western Vale, she had laid aside the blue wool and was starting afresh with a warm, rich red.

She had been quite unable to get the abject poverty of the Frost household out of her mind, and somehow the picture of neglected little Coral had stayed with her most vividly. Julie had seen neglected little girls before. They had come to Roselinden like that, but in no time at all they'd been bathed and put into clean clothing and their old rags had gone down to the incinerator; and, with their hair trimmed and shoes polished, Miss Blake had often said that you wouldn't have known them for the same children. But no such transformation was likely for poor, pathetic little Coral.

Julie had known instinctively that she must not offer money to Hazel. She had not even been sure that Mrs. Loch would approve of the knitting. But Mrs. Loch, that tireless labourer for good causes, had, surprisingly, encouraged her.

"It is a very charitable thought," she said graciously.

"Come to me if you have any difficulties. Choose a shade which will not easily soil and try to find a pattern which requires no buttons or other fasteners. People of that kind will not sew them on again if once they come off."

Julie, amazed as usual at Mrs. Loch's instant grip of the intricacies of the situation, had done as she was told. A plain pattern with a neat polo neckline had been easily found, and Mrs. Loch's promise of help was tucked away in the back of Julie's mind. She sat now in the early afternoon sunshine on the back verandah, prepared to enjoy and make good use of her precious free hours. Working for Mrs. Loch was not hard but it was constant. More than once Julie had caught herself thinking of Marguerite's reference to "full-time service". This was it, so far as Julie was concerned.

A little furrow creased her brow as she thought of Marguerite. Marguerite was upset about something. Julie had no idea as to what it was, but it was something to do with a letter that had come in the morning's mail. She hoped it wasn't bad news. Julie finished her row and held the tape measure against her work. Nearly an inch. That was good. She'd only bought the wool yesterday afternoon. Her thoughts turned to poor little Coral.

Marguerite, hunched on the bed in her own room with a magazine open but unread before her, and a big yellow apple in her hand, munched and meditated rebelliously. Her mother was unfair. Completely unfair. Utterly unfair. Her mother had all the wrong ideas, but no power on earth would make her see that. Marguerite bit into the apple sharply, finished it and put the core on top of the bookcase beside the bed— Julie would pick it up, next morning. David had asked such a little thing, such a very little thing, and her mother had said "NO".

She reached for David's letter and read it again. There was surely nothing in the letter itself which prejudiced her mother. The notepaper looked quite impressive, with David's name and address printed into the church letterhead.

"Dear Miss Loch," David had written,

"We are having an evening service in our little church at Western Vale on the first Sunday in April at seven fifteen p.m. I would be most grateful if you would consent to sing for us on that occasion. A simple hymn would fit in most appropriately with our usual order of service. The message in the words is the thing that counts.

I do hope that it will be possible for you to come and help us in this way.

Yours in His glad Service,
David Sterling."

It was scarcely more than a business letter. Marguerite got up quickly. She would speak to her mother again.

"You are too prone to make sudden friendships," Mrs. Loch said crisply. "I could not permit you to go under any consideration."

"But it's a church service, Mummy. Julie could go with me."

"That would make no difference to my feelings, Marguerite. We do not know this Mr. Sterling, and that is sufficient reason for my attitude to his invitation."

"But, Mummy——" Marguerite stopped short. It was impossible to tell her mother that it was as if they'd known one another always. "We know a lot of the same people. He's known Mr. Cartwright for years."

"That," said Mrs. Loch, "may be small recommendation."

"Mummy! That's not—not kind." She had blundered, of course, Marguerite told herself. She shouldn't have named Mr. Cartwright. Her mother didn't care for him, or, for that matter, for anything connected with Deveringham Road. She had been to hear him once only, and then he had ruffled her sense of fitness very considerably by preaching the plain and simple Gospel as if he had been preaching it directly at *her*. Mrs. Loch was not accustomed to that. Now she realised, as soon as the words had been spoken, that she *had* been unkind; but it was not in the nature of Mrs. Loch to apologise. She took up the book which she had temporarily put aside.

"We shall consider the matter closed," she said firmly. "I will ask your father to write and decline on your behalf."

That, Marguerite felt, was the last straw. The very last straw. She betook herself to her father.

"Can't you speak to Mummy?" she implored. "She'll listen to *you*, Daddy."

Mr. Loch considered.

D

"It can't mean a lot to you, Daisybud," he said slowly. "You get so many invitations. There's no point in making an issue of it. I *would* speak to your mother," he added, with a smile which somehow took her into his confidence, "if I thought that she was wrong. But she isn't. She's right."

Marguerite sighed deeply. She could say no more. The whole afternoon, like her whole life, stretched barrenly before her. All brightness lay behind her. There was no future. Even the brown hat of the deaconess seemed unbecoming . . . .

"Let's go and have a look at the cricket," her father suggested. "They're playing at Campbell Park to-day. We can be there in five minutes."

"Who's playing who?" she asked listlessly.

"St. Cuthbert's versus someone or the other. Perhaps Julie might like to come down for an hour or so."

"I could ask her," Marguerite said without enthusiasm.

She had never been particularly interested in cricket, although both Underwood Stacey, who was the wicket-keeper for St. Cuthbert's, and Stuart Meredith, who was one of Deveringham Road's best bats, had tried on more than one occasion to give her some idea of what she was missing. Her father was a keen supporter of St. Cuthbert's team, and sometimes she had felt that the Deveringham Road boys talked of little else; but in Marguerite herself little enthusiasm had been aroused. She went in search of Julie.

"I'll have to be back by four o'clock," Julie said

dubiously. "And I'm really very anxious to get on with my knitting."

"Daddy will run you back," Marguerite promised, in the casual manner of one who offers benefits which will be bestowed by someone else. "And you can take your knitting." She went, disinterestedly, to slip into a fresh frock and to twist her curls into a luminous frame for the face that had somehow lost its light. She wondered if David played cricket.

Everyone, it seemed, was at the cricket ground. Marguerite was very slightly cheered to find that the opposing team was none other than Deveringham Road itself. She hoped that they would win. The cricket season was drawing to a close, and both St. Cuthbert's and Deveringham Road were so near to the top in the district churches' competition that it promised to be a tense match. Both teams had attracted many on-lookers, and the pleasant parkland, with the white-clad players etched against the green, presented a picture which was entirely satisfying to Mr. Loch, stimulating to Marguerite, and quite new to Julie.

Marguerite, drawing Julie with her, was immediately absorbed into a laughing, chatting, excited group. The game was on, but not one move did Julie understand. She knew that Marguerite, exchanging bright patter with the young folk from Deveringham Road, would not miss her. She slipped away and sat, her back against the white fence, on a green cushion of grass. She took out her knitting. The days were getting colder, and little half-clad Coral would need some woollies.

A young fellow of her own age, immaculate in flannels, and with a sheaf of blue papers in his hand, came and, surprisingly, sat down beside her.

"I was wondering if you'd like a registration form for our Christian Endeavour house-party," he said with friendly directness. "We have one every year—most of the young people from Deveringham Road go to it—we have some super times. You're a friend of Marguerite's, aren't you? I've seen you with her at church."

Julie smiled at him shyly. He was a lad of most ordinary appearance, yet there was something wholesome and very likeable about him.

"I've seen you, too," she acknowledged. "I'm Julie Westaway."

"And I'm Bill Meredith. Stuart's brother. I expect you've met Stuart."

"Yes. I think he and Marguerite are friends."

Bill grinned. "Stuart would like to think so," he said. "That's Stuart batting for us, of course. The one without the cap. He always opens up for Deveringham Road, and if he gets set he'll be there all the afternoon. That's why I'm handing out these registration forms. Stuart only got them from the duplicating people this morning—he's secretary for the house-party, you see. I'm not likely to be batting before next Saturday, unless our side collapses—I'm always last man in!" He laughed cheerfully. "D'you like cricket, Julie?"

"I don't know. I've never seen it played."

Bill was shocked. "Something will have to be done about *that*," he said firmly.

At ten minutes to four Julie got up, regretfully. She would have to walk home, of course. Mr. Loch had no doubt completely forgotten her existence. Mrs. Loch had magnanimously said that she could have an extra half-hour if she wished, her tone implying that no-one would actually *wish* to stay and watch a cricket match unless they had nothing better to do. But it had, for Julie, been a very happy little experience. For the first time since leaving Roselinden she had felt herself to be part of a community, for one of Bill's friends had joined them, and two or three of the quieter Deveringham Road girls, and in a way which she could not have explained they had drawn her into the fellowship of their circle. They begged her to register for the house-party. She'd love it, they said. She could not promise—it was something of which Mrs. Loch might strongly disapprove—but to Julie it meant a great deal to know that these natural, friendly young folk wanted to have her with them.

To Bill and to one of the girls, Helen Spencer, she felt especially drawn, for both had that special, indefinable something which characterised Marguerite and David Sterling, and which she invariably connected in her mind with old Mr. Rose. She looked across at Marguerite and her heart rejoiced. Marguerite was happy again, the most animated of all the animated group of girls who laughed and clapped and held their breath as Stuart Meredith hit boundary after boundary for Deveringham Road. She did not even notice Julie, quietly walking away from the pleasant scene and back to her responsibilities. . . .

Stuart Meredith batted magnificently. He saw six other wickets fall before in an unguarded moment he snicked the ball into the waiting and almost unbelieving hands of Underwood Stacey when his score stood at one hundred and twenty-three. The Deveringham Road supporters almost lost their heads with excited pride. They shook his hand, they thumped him on the back, the more exuberant of the younger girls almost embarrassed him with their expressions of hero-worship. Within ten minutes play had closed for the day.

Stuart lingered beside his bicycle. No triumph or elation could completely overcome his natural shyness, but the success of the afternoon had inspired him with a temerity of which he was determined to make the most. He waited until he could have a word with Marguerite alone.

"I have some new records," he said. "Male voice, and the Messiah. I wondered if you'd care to come around to-night and hear them. I could pick you up about eight."

She scarcely thanked him. A lock of his dark hair had fallen across his forehead and in an abstracted sort of way she wished that he would brush it back into place. The excitement of the game was over, and she was fast coming down to earth again.

"Not to-night," she said carelessly. "I want to get to bed early."

He looked after her wistfully. Oh well. That was what you got for growing up with a girl. She simply didn't know that you existed.

CHAPTER ELEVEN

THERE was a visiting preacher at St. Cuthbert's. There was nothing particularly inspiring about him, and the minds of two members of the Loch family had no difficulty whatsoever in going off on missions of their own. Mrs. Loch, however, listened intently.

She made a point of concentrating on the sermon each Sunday morning, for she had the rare gift of shutting her mind to all that should be without. The preaching at St. Cuthbert's was entirely to Mrs. Loch's taste. On no occasion did it disturb her peace of mind or awaken from sleep her comfortable beliefs. The preacher on this particular morning might even have known that Mrs. Loch was present, for he spoke on the text "She hath done what she could" and gave great commendation to those whose works were sacrificial and charitable.

The light from the jewelled glory of a stained-glass window fell directly across the preacher and the beautiful piece of craftsmanship which was the pulpit. But Marguerite saw nothing of the familiar beauty of St. Cuthbert's. By screwing up her eyes in a certain way she found that she could make the preacher look quite different. He was middle-aged, as old as her father; but he was tall and neatly-built, and, by the creating of a form of optical illusion, she was able to make his figure seem almost boyish—and, by the trickery of light and the exercise of some imagination, it was possible to believe that his head (which bore little hair of any colour at all) was red.

Marguerite sighed. Two seats ahead of her sat Underwood Stacey, with his mother, his sister, and his maiden aunt. His hair was brown, a nondescript brown, and he wore an impeccably tailored suit of what seemed almost the same colour. He was, she decided, the least interesting person in the whole of her acquaintance. She sighed again. It was a very small sigh, but her father, sitting beside her, heard it. He shot a quick glance at her.

She looked pensive. He wondered why. Marguerite should never look pensive. Marguerite should shine. She had been very quiet, withdrawn, since the little incident about the invitation to sing at Western Vale. That wasn't like Marguerite, either. He had never known her to bear a grudge. And her mother was right. Quite right.

A sudden idea flashed into his mind, but he pushed it quickly aside because it was unbidden and unwelcome. He looked straight ahead of him and into the back of Underwood Stacey.

No-one would have guessed, seeing him sitting there with all his female relations, that he was St. Cuthbert's only good wicket-keeper. He was, Mr. Loch supposed, what would be known as a dutiful son. His mind went off to the match of yesterday, seeing again the superb strokes of young Meredith, the determined bowling which had quite failed to find his wicket, the neat way in which the dutiful Underwood had taken that catch behind; and he was on his feet singing, with the dirge-like mournfulness peculiar to St. Cuthbert's, while his mind was still back on the outer edge of the cricket field with his own cronies, praising or belittling each move as befitted those who were now themselves too old for play. . . .

He suddenly remembered that he was still in church. Mrs. Loch was singing two words behind Marguerite. "Go, labour on; spend, and be spent . . ." He wondered why Mrs. Loch looked so gratified. With the close of the service he made straight for Underwood Stacey, congratulating him.

Julie had the lunch ready, the table daintily and faultlessly set. Mrs. Loch's mind registered approval, but she did not go so far as to express it. Julie was a fortunate girl, a very fortunate girl. Mrs. Loch took her hat off, smoothed the petals of the crimson rose which adorned it, and put it carefully away in tissue paper. Mrs. Stacey had a new hat, she'd noticed. That was rather foolish, so late in the season. Rather extravagant, too, with so many good causes crying out for help, as that very discerning preacher had pointed out. She put the hat away in its proper place. Mrs. Loch's church-going was over for the day.

Upstairs in her room, lovingly tidied by Julie in her absence, Marguerite kicked off her black suede shoes and pushed them, on their sides, under the bed with her foot. She felt utterly frustrated. She wished that she had the courage to tell her mother and father that she never wanted to go to St. Cuthbert's again. St. Cuthbert's was beautiful but for her it was dead. One of these days she, Marguerite Loch, would sing right ahead of both the organ and the choir and *then* she would be in disgrace. It was all so different, so alive at Deveringham Road. That was where David would fit in. She couldn't, despite her imaginings, picture David at St. Cuthbert's. The whole burden of her parents' injustice rolled over her afresh.

Downstairs, Mr. Loch, buoyed up by the savoury smells which were soon to leave the kitchen for the dining-room, looked squarely at the idea which had presented itself to him and found that it was, after all, not unacceptable.

"I've been thinking, Gwen," he said. "About this invitation Marguerite received yesterday. It wouldn't be bad experience for her. Would it make any difference to your feelings if I went out with the girls myself?"

For the third time in the month of March David Sterling ground his faithful Aspidistra to a halt in the vicinity of Number Seven, Crossley Road. He was careful to call first at Number Five. Mrs. Featherberry would certainly hear about it if he visited the undeserving Mrs. Frost and neglected that shining pattern of Guild ladies, Mrs. McGlynn. Mrs. McGlynn, however, was not at home.

David was rather relieved. It saved him from having to name a reason for calling. Mrs. McGlynn would almost certainly suspect such sudden pastoral care. He had no such misgivings regarding his call on Mrs.

Frost, for he had a reason, an excellent reason, a pearl among reasons, for visiting her again so soon.

"I have come to invite you to our church service next Sunday evening," he said pleasantly, when Hazel answered his knock.

She shrugged her shoulders. "You need a lot of telling, Mr. Sterling. I told you before that I wouldn't go."

He was conveniently hard of hearing. "It will be a rather special service, Mrs. Frost. Miss Marguerite Loch is coming to sing for us."

"I'm still not going."

"Julie will be coming with her, I understand."

"So what?"

"Julie would like to see you, Mrs. Frost, I'm sure. Mr. Loch is bringing the girls out by car. He 'phoned this morning to confirm arrangements. You'd like to see Julie, wouldn't you?"

"You win," she said shortly. "I'd like to see Julie. But I'm still not going to church."

David hesitated. Something more than mere indifference lay behind this. "Is there any particular reason?" he asked gently.

She made the age-old plea, but in this case it was genuine enough. "I haven't anything fit to wear."

"God doesn't look upon the outward appearance, Mrs. Frost."

She laughed mirthlessly. "You can say that again. He'd see to it that I had some decent clothes if He did."

He thought of the lilies of the field, of the gracious, lovely promises of Matthew chapter six, but some instinct which was deeper than his boyish inexperience told him that it was not the time to speak of these things. Instead he said: "Julie would like to see you. And Marguerite."

"In my old blue floral with the hem hanging down?"

"In your old blue floral," he said firmly. He added, daringly: "You might be able to do something about the hem."

She was not in the least offended. "But I have no hat."

"We aren't very formal in our little church. You needn't worry about that. You *will* come, Mrs. Frost, won't you?"

"Not without a hat," she said stubbornly.

She was adamant about it. There was only one thing to be done. David turned on her his most charming smile.

"Mrs. Frost," he said proudly, "I shall *get* you a hat."

She laughed again, this time with genuine, surprised amusement. "You're a perseverer, I'll say that for you, Mr. Sterling. They always say you never know what a red-head will do next." She threw him a challenge. "Get me a hat and I'll come to church. A hat to keep, mind."

"It shall be done," he assured her gravely.

"Where will you get it?" she asked, suddenly suspicious. "Not from Mrs. McGlynn?"

Man-like, he had intended to do that very thing. Realisation of the folly of his intention almost overwhelmed him. He would have to think quickly.

"I haven't the slightest idea," he said honestly. "But

God has. Let's see. This is Tuesday. The hat shall be here by Friday afternoon."

The Reverend David Sterling had prayed for many and various things in his twenty-one years, but never before had he asked that God would provide him with a lady's hat. The extraordinary nature of his request did not in the least deter him. The Lord had answered more than one extraordinary prayer in the course of history, and there was no reason to believe that any less consideration would be given to the petitions of the Reverend David Sterling. There was, however, the little matter of ways and means.

He had learned one lesson. The hat must not be got locally. It was apparent that even Mrs. Frost had some pride. And there was one considerable difficulty. He had in his own pocket half-a-dozen florins and a handful of smaller coins. Something told him that a lady's hat would cost rather more than that.

Inspiration came to him on Wednesday evening as he looked up some references in a book lent to him by his old friend Mr. Cartwright of Deveringham Road. Mrs. Cartwright would help him. They had ministered in David's own home church during his boyhood and he had faith to believe that they had the answer to every problem. He couldn't quite see Mrs. Frost in one of Mrs. Cartwright's plain, matronly hats, but no doubt she would have a neighbour, or a friend, who could help . . . .

It was as good as settled. If he took his Scripture classes at the local school first thing on Thursday morning he could then have the rest of the day off. He would discard his clerical collar for a few hours. He hadn't treated himself to a free day for weeks—he found himself looking forward to it with real pleasure. It would be good to see Mr. Cartwright again.

His hopes were dashed but his faith was unshaken when he found the Cartwright doors locked and all the windows forbiddingly shut. Mr. Cartwright, too, must be having a day off. But God knew how important the hat was. David wondered if he might dare drive around by the Loch address. All right. If God wanted either Marguerite or Julie to help in the matter He would see to it that one or the other would be within sight as he passed. He took out his street directory.

He drove past slowly, admiring the gracious old Colonial home but seeing no-one. He drove on, scarcely knowing where, turning one corner and then another; and the hats that he saw were all prettily or crazily poised on feminine heads.

He turned yet another corner, and a lovely old church came unexpectedly into view. He pulled up without conscious intention. Any old, beautiful place of worship called to him irresistibly. The door was open, and he entered reverently, reading the name on the sign as he passed : ST. CUTHBERT'S.

He felt a warm sense of God's reality. Marguerite had mentioned St. Cuthbert's almost casually. He had no idea that it was a lovely old church like this. Someone was playing the organ, softly. 'Jesu, joy of man's desiring . . .' He knelt, worshipping.

But he did not forget the business in hand. He told God again how urgently he needed the hat. He walked out into the sunshine. There was a smaller board on the adjacent Sunday School Hall. He walked across to it, interested.

The inscription thereon was printed in chalk. He read it once and then twice, scarcely daring to believe that it told the truth. The message it bore was a simple one.

JUMBLE SALE NOW ON.

It must be admitted that the Reverend David Sterling had a rather poor idea of jumble sales as a means of raising money for the Lord's work. He'd always rather looked down on churches which employed such methods. But God used many odd things to His glory. . . .

He hesitated, swallowed hard, and walked in. The hall was quiet, the long trestle table with its motley collection of cast-off garments devoid of customers. The rush, apparently, was over. In the background sat three well-dressed, highly superior ladies, sipping tea daintily from thick white church cups. There was a fur cape over the back of one of the chairs, carefully spread. The morning had been cold, David remembered, but he supposed jumble selling was warm work. One of the highly superior ladies put down her cup and came forward.

"May I help you?" she asked graciously.

The special charm which had disarmed the critical Mrs. Featherberry, the suspicious Mrs. Frost, and even the austere Mrs. McGlynn, sprang gallantly to David's aid. "Thank you," he said. "I'm looking for a hat. For a lady."

"I'm afraid our range is rather depleted," said Mrs. Loch, in the tone of one who would say 'Our new autumn collection is not yet in'. "We were rather overwhelmed with customers this morning. Could you tell me something of your requirements?"

David couldn't. He couldn't describe Mrs. Frost's possible tastes to this very elegant lady.

"It's for church," he said inadequately.

Mrs. Loch was touched. She questioned David skilfully, discreetly, as to the lady's age, her height, her colouring. She made the final selection herself, and it says much for the power of David's personality that she chose for him one of her own exclusive, discarded models which she had put aside for a special protegée of hers who was expected to call in later in the afternoon.

"That will be one and sixpence," she said regally.

He handed her a two-shilling piece. With great dignity she gave him his change and put the hat into a paper bag which had 'Madame Celestine' printed on its side. She went back to her seat and poured herself another cup of tea.

"What a charming young man!" she said to Mrs. Stacey. "What a *very* charming young man!"

CHAPTER TWELVE

IT was Miss Blake's birthday. It is possible that Miss Levering knew how old Miss Blake was, but it was very certain that no-one else at Roselinden had ever succeeded in finding it out. Miss Blake, like Roselinden, was an institution and, therefore, ageless. The girls at Cottage Two got over the difficulty by putting one candle on the birthday cake year by year.

It had always been a happy day, Julie remembered, with a special tea and presents, and the added joy of an evening hour of fun arranged by the girls themselves. She was going to miss that part of it. Last year she and Lexie had arranged the games. She did not spend a lot of time in thinking about Roselinden, but she knew that she would never really have it far from her mind and heart; and it was good that she could slip back and see Miss Blake on this very special occasion. She could have an hour or so with her, during the afternoon, and perhaps she might even be able to do some little thing towards the birthday tea.

She paused at the sitting-room door on her way out. She was at liberty to go wherever she wished during her free time, but Mrs. Loch had asked that, as a precaution, she always inform someone where she intended to go before leaving. Julie, accustomed to the rigid rules of Roselinden, saw nothing but good sense in this. Mrs. Loch was not at home, but she knew that

Marguerite was at the piano. She knocked on the door softly.

Marguerite, turning the pages of her hymn-book at random and playing a few bars here and there, was pleased to see her.

"I'm looking for something to sing on Sunday night," she told Julie. "Isn't Daddy the most surprising darling? It would never have occurred to me that he'd suggest taking us out to Western Vale himself."

It would never have occurred to Julie, either, but she was beginning to learn that she was not always expected to reply to Marguerite's statements or even to her questions.

"I expect Hazel will be there," Marguerite went on. "It will be nice to see Hazel again, won't it?"

"She told me that she never went to church," Julie said apologetically.

"Mr. Sterling suggested something simple. Julie, do you think that this is *too* simple? I've just found another tune to it. 'Westminster New'." She played a soft chord or two.

Julie, who had only recently discovered that hymn tunes had names, and was quite at a loss to know how Marguerite could remember which belonged to which, nodded obligingly.

"Whatever you choose will be the right one," she said loyally.

Softly Marguerite sang :

> *O Jesus Christ, grow Thou in me,*
> *And all things else recede.*

Effortlessly she slid on to the closing lines of another verse:

> O let the glow of Thy great love
> Through my whole being shine.

"It does," Julie whispered. "Marguerite, it does."

She stopped short, almost shocked at the spoken revelation of her own soul. She had put into words that which for weeks she had been putting into action, her almost worshipful love for Marguerite.

Marguerite was touched. "I'm glad," she said simply. She turned another page or so. "Maybe I won't look any further now. I think that's the one." She looked at Julie and, for the first time, noticed the little parcel, gaily wrapped, in Julie's hand.

"Are you going out, Julie?" she asked.

"I'm going to Roselinden to see Miss Blake. It's her birthday to-day."

Marguerite's interest was captured immediately. "I've always wanted to see Roselinden. Inside, I mean. I think I'll come with you, Julie, if you don't mind. I haven't anything particular to do. Mummy was so busy getting away to the jumble sale that she quite overlooked the little matter of giving me a job." She laughed at the remembrance of something that had struck her as being deliciously amusing. "She almost suggested that I might go along and help her!"

Had anyone other than Marguerite made the suggestion regarding the visit to Miss Blake Julie would have minded very much indeed. She had been looking forward to a quiet hour with Miss Blake. She had so much to tell her. About Hazel, especially. But this was Marguerite.

"I'd love you to come," she said sincerely.

Marguerite was already on her feet, scattering her music, lifting a handful of late Radiance rosebuds from a vase and sprinkling water on the polished table. "A piece of cellophane, Julie, please," she ordered happily. "These will make a lovely birthday bouquet for Miss Blake, won't they? I'll be ready in two seconds." She ran off, singing as she went:

> O let the glow of Thy great love
> Through my whole being shine.

Julie gathered up the music and closed the piano. She mopped up the water and made a posy of the flowers. Miss Blake *would* be pleased. She was at the front door when Marguerite came down, a lovely, shining picture in a new primrose-coloured jacket and slim grey skirt. They turned their steps towards Rose-linden.

They found Miss Blake in anything but a birthday mood.

She had a headache, and she was also very cross. It was staff trouble again, she told Julie.

"Those young girls!" she said scornfully, as if Julie were a middle-aged woman and well able to understand the unreliability of youth. "One last week and another this morning!"

"Who were they?" Julie asked, instantly comprehending that which meant nothing at all to the listening Marguerite.

"You wouldn't know the one who went last week. She had been *called* to the work, she said. She stayed exactly eight days," Miss Blake said with heavy sarcasm. "She was quite surprised to find that she had to soil her hands. It was that Miss Terry who went this morning. She was transferred across from Three, the week after you left. *Then* it was Mrs. Lang who felt she'd made a mistake in her vocation. Her *vocation*," repeated Miss Blake witheringly. "She was the poorest cook I ever had to put up with." She sighed hopelessly. "Miss Levering interviewed another one this morning. All lipstick and dangling ear-rings and heels you'd break your back over!"

Marguerite was fascinated and, for once, silent. She had never given any practical thought to the inner workings of Roselinden. She had just taken it for granted that the ladies' committee was all-powerful, in view of the fact that her mother was one of its members; and it had never entered her head that there would not be a willing queue of Miss Blakes, already in neat grey uniforms, in the background always. It had never occurred to her, either, that members of the Roselinden staff might be even comparatively *young*. This was all most interesting. She saw the harassed look leave Miss Blake's face as Julie, just by being herself, smoothed down the ruffled spirit.

"I'll make a cup of tea," Miss Blake said. "Julie, you just run across and see Miss Levering while I get it ready. She'd like to see you." She added significantly: "You'd best not look at the brass vase while you're there. *That* Daffodil Baker. . . ."

The office block stood next to Cottage Two, so close that Miss Blake's girls had always been responsible for its cleaning and polishing. Julie's thoughts were busy as she climbed the familiar stairs. She came on to the landing and her first glance was for the big brass bowl. It overflowed with Easter daisies and late dahlias but it really did look dreadful, with the polish only half-rubbed out of the complicated embossing. Daffodil Baker must be even worse than she'd imagined. Julie's fingers itched for a good soft cloth. She knocked on Miss Levering's door.

Miss Levering was, as always, perfectly calm and beautifully correct. "I'm very pleased to see you, Julie," she said. "Could you wait for just one moment, please?"

The long seat with the quaint carved ends was empty. Julie sat down, more for old times' sake than for any real need to sit. She had no fear now of any news which Miss Levering might have to impart. She was just glad that she was glad to be there. She lifted her eyes, and there, as shabby and inartistic as ever, was Mr. Rose's text.

'My God shall supply all your need according to His riches in glory by Christ Jesus.'

Something within her suddenly leapt, rejoicing. It was true. It had happened. Already. It had happened to *her*, Julie Westaway, even while she was wondering how it *could* happen. The sheer wonder of it swept over her like a wave. She'd seen those words, every day, in her own little pink room at Mrs. Loch's; but it had taken Mr. Rose's text itself to bring her to realisation of the amazing and wonderful way in which God *had* supplied all her need. He had even brought Hazel back into her life for some purpose. In her moment of illumination she dimly saw what that purpose was. She, who had received so much, needed someone to whom she could give. . . .

The moment passed. 'By Christ Jesus.' That was the difficult part. Julie sighed. God had done so much for her, but she still did not know Him. . . .

Ten minutes later she was back at Cottage Two. Miss Levering had been most kind. She had even mentioned that Mrs. Loch had reported satisfaction with Julie's work. She had asked if Julie needed anything, but Julie had shaken her head. "I have everything," she said simply.

She found Marguerite busy putting out Miss Blake's own private tea set with the painted carnations on the cups and saucers. She was chattering ceaselessly and happily, and Miss Blake was smiling. The rosebuds were in a crystal vase on the table. Miss Blake had, without a doubt, been won. Julie's heart swelled with happiness and pride.

They talked about Hazel when the cups and saucers had been taken back to the kitchen and Miss Blake had resignedly taken the mending basket from its shelf. There were buttons off everywhere, she complained, and the sewing ladies weren't due for another week. Julie took up a needle and cotton, Marguerite did likewise. Miss Blake set a tin of pearl buttons and a pile of school blouses on the table. "And was Mrs. Frost pleased to see you?" she asked.

Marguerite's mind went off in another direction. She was intrigued to find that a name was marked inside the neck-band of each blouse. E. Carrigan. F. Rowe. C. Miller. Marguerite, who looked upon the sewing on of buttons as a form of the most extreme self-discipline, found her mind soaring beyond the necessity for giving direction to needle and cotton. What did the E and the F and the C represent? She hoped that they were pretty names. Little orphan girls needed pretty names. They needed everything, really. She would have liked to question Miss Blake, but the delicate subject of the apparent shortcomings of Mr. Andrew Frost was under discussion and she did not like to interrupt. She looked at Miss Blake.

Thirty years she'd been at Roselinden, she said. You could do a lot of things for a lot of girls in thirty years. You could sew on a lot of buttons. She realised guiltily that she hadn't even threaded her needle although she had C. Miller's blouse in her hand. It looked as if C. must be hard on buttons, too. Marguerite's thoughts turned back to herself.

To sing for the Lord was a great privilege. To be able to sing for Him at Western Vale was a great opportunity. David had told her that so few of the people who came to his services really knew Him. She had at first been a little sorry that David had asked for something simple, but she saw now that anything showy would be out of place. Julie's words had made up her mind for her. It was sweet of Julie to say what she did. To shine with the glow of the Lord was the greatest privilege of all.

It was *her* hymn, and she would sing it. For Julie. For David Sterling. For the Lord. She began to hum softly to herself, and the tune that she hummed was 'Westminster New'.

CHAPTER THIRTEEN

HAZEL closed the front door stealthily behind her and slipped out through the ever-open gate with the wariness of a cat. Andy had flatly forbidden her to go to church, but she was going just the same. It would mean a row, of course, but rows were as familiar to Hazel as the dirt on the front steps. She had made a promise to the parson boy, and she was going to keep it, Andy or no Andy.

She hadn't thought for one moment that he'd get that hat for her. And such a hat! It wasn't so much the shape or the colour that took the eye. It was the one handsome bronze chrysanthemum which adorned it and for which Mrs. Loch had been most happy to pay quite a fabulous sum. To Hazel, that bronze chrysanthemum represented the dizziest heights of luxury. She hadn't dared let Andy catch sight of it, or of the paper bag with 'Madame Celestine' printed on it. She'd bring it out one day and tell Andy that Mrs. Brown at the farm across the road had given it to her. She had never spoken to Mrs. Brown, but Andy would believe anything, if she caught him at the right moment, and he wasn't proud when it came to receiving benefactions from those more favoured than himself. But he'd draw the line at a parson boy. . . .

The big grey Customline pulled up at the little church just ahead of her. Hazel knew without any telling that it must belong to Marguerite's father. There weren't many cars like that in Western Vale. She drew back into the shadows and watched the three move up to the door and out of sight. The slighter girl was Julie, of course. A difficult lump came into Hazel's throat. Alan's girl. Her step-daughter. And, a mile away, in a home which could be called nothing better than squalid, was Andy. . . .

The man who served behind the counter at the grocer's gave Hazel a hymnbook and shook hands with her. She took the book and moved on hurriedly. She hadn't been able to improve her position with the grocer but she hadn't come to church to be reminded of *that*. It was early. There were very few people in the little church, and she slipped into an inconspicuous corner seat against the wall. She would have liked to sit with Julie, but that was quite out of the question. Even the bronze chrysanthemum didn't make it right for her to embarrass Julie in front of her grand friends. . . .

She sat down hesitantly. She hadn't been to church since she married Andy. Alan hadn't been much of a church-goer, either, but he wasn't dead against it like Andy. She wondered if Andy had discovered her absence yet. . . .

It was a simple service, as simple and unpretentious as the building in which it was held. It made a tremendous appeal to Julie because it took nothing for granted. She was beginning to love Deveringham Road, but she could not overcome her feeling that everyone else there was so far ahead of her in their acquaintance with God. She soon saw that this service at Western Vale was for beginners.

The words of the first hymn were so familiar that she did not have to look at her book. 'Tell me the old, old story . . .' They'd sung it at Roselinden dozens of times. But no-one at Roselinden had ever prayed as David prayed now. Julie liked his prayer because, like old Mr. Cartwright, he talked to God as if he knew Him, but, better still, as if he were taking everyone in the congregation and leading them, by the hand, into His Presence. She could almost feel David's hand in hers, helping her into understanding, and there was nothing unnatural in the thought. He opened his Bible.

"Our reading this evening will be taken from the Gospel according to St. John, chapter fourteen, verses one to fourteen," he said.

The folk at Deveringham Road took their Bibles to church with them; but Julie heard no rustling of pages behind her now. Perhaps most of the people at Western Vale didn't even have Bibles. She herself had no difficulty in finding the place. One of the Sunday School teachers at Roselinden had so drilled the girls in the books of the Old and New Testaments that she couldn't possibly forget them. But she didn't watch the words. She watched, instead, the face of David Sterling.

She supposed that she had probably heard those verses before, but never had she heard them read as David read them now. He made them sound as if they meant something. He looked older, more mature, in his dark suit, and all the nonsense and light-heartedness had fallen away from him and he was utterly in earnest.

" 'Thomas saith unto Him'," read David, " 'Lord, we know not whither Thou goest; and how can we know the way? Jesus saith unto him, I am the way, the truth, and the life: no man cometh unto the Father, but by Me . . .' "

He read to the end of the fourteenth verse, closed his Bible, and paused. There was the quietness of a cathedral in the plain little church.

"Miss Marguerite Loch will now sing for us," he said.

Julie's heart thrilled. Marguerite. Mr. Loch must be proud of her. She had never looked lovelier. She wore a new autumn suit of soft green wool and her honey-gold curls formed an enchanting brim for her tiny white hat; but things like that didn't seem to matter. It was Marguerite herself who was important.

No. Not just Marguerite herself. She began to sing. Julie had a moment's nervousness. The thin lady at the organ didn't seem any too sure of 'Westminster New'. By the end of the first verse Julie knew that that didn't matter, either. Nothing mattered but the sure knowledge that Someone was speaking, shining, appealing, through Marguerite.

Marguerite herself knew no nervousness. She was accustomed to singing in public. She had given considerable thought to the hymn, wondering at first if some of the six verses might be deleted; but she decided against that. The verses were very short, and they were also inseparable. God had guided her choice, and she must sing it as it had been written. But, as she faced the congregation and saw them for the first time, something happened. For a split second she had the foolish impression that the woman in the corner seat near the back was her mother.

Marguerite knew that she would recognise that bronze chrysanthemum anywhere. Her mother always bought what she believed to be exclusive hats, and this was one of two summers ago. Marguerite recognised the mistake as soon as she had made it. Of course it wasn't her mother. She hadn't worn that hat for ages. It was another woman with the same sort of hat. Her mother wouldn't have been pleased about that, especially in a place like Western Vale. With the next moment she knew that the woman, shabby except for the hat, was Hazel.

She came to the third verse, the thought of her mother still strangely close to her mind. She was proud of her mother, and deeply fond of her, but she knew that they did not understand one another. There was a strain of wistfulness in her voice as she finished the fourth verse.

> *I would Thy living image be,*
> *In joy and sorrow too.*

It was difficult to make her mother understand. The nearer she herself drew to the Lord the less close she seemed to her mother. But all things were possible with God. He would straighten that out, in His own good time. The wistfulness disappeared, and smilingly she put her whole heart into the next verse.

Fill me with gladness from above,
Hold me by strength divine!
Lord, let the glow of Thy great love
Through my whole being shine.

She almost whispered the last verse, yet, in the hush of the little church, each word was clear and telling.

Make this poor self grow less and less,
Be Thou my life and aim;
Oh, make me daily, through Thy grace,
More meet to bear Thy name!

David rose to his feet. He had not been able to see Marguerite's face, but he had seen two other faces and they had spoken for themselves. The reflected light in Julie's, the hunger in Hazel's, told him all that he needed to know. He had at first wondered if Marguerite's choice would altogether fit in with his own thoughts in the address; and then he knew that it would, for, while he himself was seeking to lead people to God, Marguerite sang as one who had already found Him.

David did not thank her as she went back to her seat. Something told him that, instead, he should thank God. "Let us all pray," he said quietly.

Ten minutes later he announced his text. "I am the way, the truth, and the life: no man cometh unto the Father but by Me."

It was a simple sermon. David had commonsense. He knew how much most of his hearers would understand. Mr. Loch was impressed, Marguerite delighted;

but to Julie and to Hazel his words came as the very words for which, unconsciously, they had been waiting. They came as from God Himself.

From the first words Julie had no doubt in her mind. David was going to clear up her problems. God, who had so wonderfully supplied all her need, was about to supply that something more which would put everything into its right place. She had never been more certain of anything.

The story of the Cross had always awed her. She had heard it year by year at Roselinden, and the thought of the sufferings of the Son of God had pained her dreadfully, for He was so good, so gentle, so absolutely undeserving of such shameful, cruel treatment. That was just it, David said. He quoted some lines from a hymn which had always been a favourite at Roselinden:

> There was no other good enough,
>   To pay the price of sin;
> He only could unlock the gate
>   Of Heaven, and let us in.

" 'I am the way . . .'," David repeated. " 'No man cometh unto the Father but by Me.' " He turned the pages of his Bible. "There are some words in the first Epistle of Peter, chapter three, verse eighteen, which will help us to understand just why Jesus went to the Cross. 'For Christ also hath once suffered for sins, the just for the unjust, that He might bring us to God.' "

That He might bring us to God, Julie's heart repeated. David had made it so plain that God wanted everyone to come to Him, but someone had to bring them, and the Someone Whom He had chosen had been His own Son, Jesus Christ. People weren't good enough to come by themselves, David said. That was what it meant when it said that Christ had suffered for sins, the just for the unjust, that He might bring them to God. . . .

The thing to do, David said, was first to *believe* that Christ had done this wonderful, amazing thing for *you*, personally, and then to put your hand into *His* hand, trusting Him, going along with Him because He was the Way and because no-one could come unto the Father but by Him. It was as simple and as marvellous as that, David said.

He closed his Bible. For one moment he hesitated. There was something different in the church to-night. He had sensed it from the beginning, and Marguerite's singing had deepened it. He knew that God expected him to do something more, and it was something that he had never before done.

"It may be," he said simply, "that there is someone in this church to-night who is seeking God through Jesus Christ Who is the Way. It may be that there is someone who has found Him. It would help you very much if now, in the quietness of this service, you were to stand for one moment to acknowledge your desire to put your hand into His and to go out of this church *with Him*." He paused. "It would help you very much," he repeated.

Julie knew what she should do. It had been exactly as she had expected. David had explained everything

E

so clearly. She knew that she still had much to learn, but she as surely knew that she had made a beginning. She knew that Christ had died for her, for Julie Westaway, that He might bring her to God. "All had sinned," David had assured them. The Word of God said so. "But," David had added triumphantly, "the blood of Jesus Christ His Son cleanseth us from all sin . . . If we confess our sins, He is faithful and just to forgive us our sins, and to cleanse us from all unrighteousness."

There was no doubt whatsoever in Julie's mind. God would forgive her and cleanse her and accept her as His own because Jesus Christ His Son had died for her. She felt that her hand had slipped out of David's into the hand of Christ Himself, and because of that she had at last found God. There was a quiet, grateful joy in her heart; but she did not stand. All her native shyness, her inborn reserve, held her to her seat.

She couldn't do it. Not here. Not in front of all these strangers. Not in front of Mr. Loch. In her own heart she knew that she had found her way to God. Surely that was all that mattered. Some day, perhaps, she might be able to tell David, if there was a quiet opportunity. She heard him speak to someone behind her. Someone must have stood. Had she been at Deveringham Road it would have been different, she told herself. She couldn't do it here. She just couldn't.

"Our closing hymn," David said, "will be number three hundred and fifty-three."

Julie could not sing. She could not look at David. She just wanted to get outside. David would want to

speak to Marguerite—she herself could just slip quietly
away and wait by the car. It was most unlikely that
Hazel would be present. Julie made something of a fuss
of collecting her hymnbook and Bible when the Benediction was over. She knew that she couldn't look at
Marguerite, either.

She saw the bronze chrysanthemum as soon as she
turned, and for one moment her mind was deflected
from herself. This was Hazel, sitting motionless, her
eyes fixed on her ungloved hands, her poor attire
contrasting sharply with the hat that was on her head.
She did not look up. Quietly, almost stealthily, Julie
passed the end of the seat. She knew now that she
would not see Hazel to talk to to-night. She also knew
that she had never before felt so utterly and completely miserable.

The man from the grocer's gathered up the
hymnbooks and carried the collection plate into the
little room at the back, where the husband of the
organist was waiting to help him count its contents.
The little church was quiet. David came in from the
porch on tiptoe, knowing that he walked on holy
ground. He had had no time for more than a formal
handshake and brief word with Marguerite and Julie.
He was disappointed, very disappointed; but he knew
where he was needed. He slipped into the seat beside
Hazel. She lifted her head and looked at him candidly.

"It wasn't so much what you said that did it," she
told him. "It was the look on Marguerite's face when
she was singing. She seemed to be singing straight at
me."

CHAPTER FOURTEEN

THE week that followed was difficult for everyone.

Julie awakened on the Monday morning in a thoroughly dejected frame of mind. She felt that she had disappointed both God and Marguerite, and she could see no way of making amends. Perhaps she had even disappointed David, too. Her mind was so far from her work that she over-browned the toast, an offence which Mrs. Loch considered almost unforgivable.

"I am afraid that your thoughts are wandering this morning, Julie," she said in a voice which was as crisp as the toast itself.

"I'm sorry," Julie apologised. Mrs. Loch was always so right. Of course her thoughts were wandering. She went back to the kitchen and poured herself a strong cup of coffee. It was *good* coffee, but she couldn't expect Mrs. Loch to compliment her on that when the toast was too brown. She crunched her way through a slice without enjoyment.

Marguerite was still upstairs. She might even be still asleep. Julie hoped that Mrs. Loch wouldn't ask her to take up a tray. The unspoken hope shocked her, because she knew that it came from no unwillingness to serve but from her unwillingness to be alone with Marguerite. But Mrs. Loch made no such suggestion. She was not pleased with Marguerite and because of that there would be no special favours. To her husband she put this into words.

"I sometimes think we do too much for Marguerite," she stated. "She accepts too much too readily. You spoil her, of course, Philip. There was no need at all for you to take her out to that church last night, for instance. You have always said that you like your Sunday evenings at home."

Mr. Loch permitted himself a small inward smile. His wife had already made *that* quite clear. He passed his cup. "Julie makes good coffee," he commented. He stirred the sugar in slowly. "It didn't call for any particular sacrifice on my part, Gwen. I was glad to be there, as a matter of fact. Marguerite sang very nicely. I liked young Sterling. He'll go a long way, I think. By the way, Marguerite mentioned the singing lessons to me again."

"I have come to the conclusion that they would not be justified."

He was a little surprised. "She has a nice voice, Gwen. We promised the lessons as soon as she'd finished school. I'd overlooked that."

"One does not need a trained voice for the little things Marguerite sings. She has no ambition where her music is concerned. I certainly would not favour her having lessons at present, Philip. Perhaps next year, when she is at the University, and when her outlook (I hope) has been broadened, we might re-consider it."

Mr. Loch hesitated. "I am not sure that she will want to go to the University," he said slowly. "She told me last night that, if you will not finally consent to her training as a deaconess, she would like to go into Bible College next year."

"That," said Mrs. Loch crushingly, rising to her feet in order that her words might be the more impressive, "is carrying things a little *too* far."

The words were hard but the voice that spoke them quivered. Mr. Loch was instantly sorry. "This will probably pass, Gwen," he said soothingly. "Most likely she was just carried away by something that young Sterling said." He chuckled. "Did I mention that he had red hair?"

At a quarter past nine Marguerite trailed downstairs, her dressing-gown clutched around her. She had mislaid the girdle, but the pangs of hunger were so great that she did not stop to look for it. She had lingered hopefully in bed until after the clock struck nine, thinking that Julie might appear with a tray; but, as Julie did not come, it was evident that no benefits could be expected on this particular morning. She felt tired and thoroughly deflated.

The evening had been a great disappointment to her. She hadn't seen David for more than a brief word, and her prayers for Julie had not been answered. The thought of Hazel was of little comfort to her. She doubted if Hazel really understood what she was doing. She went into the empty kitchen and put two thick slices of bread into the toaster.

She could hear Julie busy with the vacuum-cleaner in the sitting-room. It was almost as if Julie didn't *want* to speak to her. She spread her toast generously with butter and honey and went in search of the *Sydney Morning Herald*.

She was in the sun-room with plate and newspaper when her mother came to her, and she sighed within herself, awaiting the words of reproof which were almost certain to come. Such were, indeed, on the tip of Mrs. Loch's tongue—had she not repeatedly told Marguerite that breakfast would be on the table at eight o'clock?—but, as she sat down and looked at her daughter, it suddenly occurred to her that the girl was not looking herself. Immediately Mrs. Loch chided herself. She had not noticed that Marguerite was pale, her young face a little drawn. She would most certainly have put a stop to that trip out to Western Vale had she not been too pre-occupied to see that the girl was not well. Something must be done about it. Swift inspiration came to her and was immediately organised into action.

"You look very tired this morning, my dear," she said gently. "I think that perhaps both you and I have been running around too much."

Marguerite was surprised and touched. She almost apologised for her lack of consideration regarding breakfast but decided that it might be best to leave well alone.

"I *am* tired," she admitted. It wasn't only tiredness of body, but she couldn't tell her mother that.

"A few days in the country would be very nice for us both. Mrs. Ferguson has invited us repeatedly, and a week or two away from our usual routine would be most refreshing. It can be quite simply arranged. I will put a 'phone call through to Mrs. Ferguson this morning and possibly we could get away on Wednesday."

Marguerite was shocked. She didn't want to go to the Fergusons. She didn't want to go away anywhere.

"But, Mummy," she objected, "I couldn't. I just couldn't. There's too much on. I have a lot of responsibilities, and there's my Sunday School class—you just can't ask me to walk out and leave them without a teacher——"

"I would not ask you to do so. I have my own church responsibilities, my dear. Sometimes I think that you overlook that. Both you and I must ask someone to deputise for us during our absence."

"But we can't just go off and leave Daddy and Julie to look after themselves!"

"That can be arranged. Your father's aunt will be happy to come and supervise things, I'm sure, and Julie is perfectly capable of keeping things comfortable for a few days. I see no obstacle which cannot be overcome. And I *want* you to come with me. The change will be good for us both."

"But I don't want to go!" Marguerite cried rebelliously. "Mummy, you don't understand!"

"I understand one thing," said Mrs. Loch, and there was a sharp edge to her words which cut remorselessly. "You find it easier to please other people than to please *me*."

There was so much truth in the statement that Marguerite for once found herself without ready reply. There *was* an answer to it, of course, but Marguerite

instinctively knew that she would do her cause no good
to tell her mother that it was impossible to please her
and the Lord at the same time. She was perfectly sure
that this move was not the Lord's will, yet she saw that,
without open conflict, there was no way of getting
out of it. Words came back to her mind, and a sudden
vision of a poorly-dressed woman with a hat like her
mother's.

> *Oh, make me daily, through Thy grace,*
> *More meet to bear Thy name!*

It was going to be hard for Hazel, too; but the way
of discipleship was never easy. "I'm sorry, Mummy,"
she said, but there was more of resignation than repentance in her tone. "I'll go with you."

For the Reverend David Sterling also the week had
started badly. He had forgotten to put out his washing
the night before, and that, in the eyes of Mrs. Featherberry, was an offence equal to the burning of toast with
Mrs. Loch. When he did remember, and apologetically
carried his bundle of shirts and socks to the laundry,
he was so plainly made to understand that Mrs. Featherberry had been much inconvenienced that he felt thoroughly chastened and entirely without excuse.

Had Mrs. Featherberry been at church on the
previous evening it is probable that she would have
been more tolerant, but her 'arthuritis' had 'taken
her sudden' and she had been obliged to stay at home
and go to bed. It was not until she attended the Guild
meeting on Tuesday afternoon that she learned that

there had been something special about the Sunday night service, and then of course it was too late to take a different attitude about the washing. On the Monday morning, with her 'arthuritis' still giving her a few twinges, she could see nothing but a bundle of shirts and socks which had come at the wrong time.

The reception given to him by his landlady had a curiously depressing effect on the Reverend David Sterling. On another occasion he would, with his natural nonsense and light-heartedness, have quickly charmed away the ire of Mrs. Featherberry. But he did not feel light-hearted. He did not really know how he felt. He did know that he was disappointed. He would have liked to have more than a brief word with the girl whose face had, for some weeks, come between him and his work. No, that was wrong. It did not come between. It drew him to it even more closely. And he was not happy about Hazel.

He had always felt that the task of the missionary must have one great advantage over that of the minister at home. Those who had never before heard the Gospel must be so glad to receive it. He had had the odd feeling that he was in somewhat similar position with Mrs. Frost. But all the difficulties lay before her. How could one begin the living of the Christian life in a household such as that of Mr. Andrew Frost? David firmly believed that 'with God all things are possible', but he knew that this was a particularly delicate situation and one in which he must turn for guidance to someone older and wiser than himself. He went to the telephone and dialled Mr. Cartwright's number.

He visited Mr. Cartwright on the Thursday afternoon. He had seen Hazel in the meantime and had
found her, as he expected, in the depths of despond-
ency, and quite convinced that she couldn't go through
with things. Some instinct told him that he must enlist
the sympathy of Mrs. Cartwright as well as that of her
husband.

He was most affectionately received. The Cart-
wrights loved him. Within ten minutes they had
restored in him a confidence which had been gradually
ebbing throughout the week. They promised to drop
all else and visit Mrs. Frost on the following day, and
then they talked of other things and especially of
Deveringham Road. Mr. Cartwright mentioned the
forthcoming Christain Endeavour house-party.

"I'd love to come," David said wistfully.

"I wish you could come, too, David," Mr. Cartwright
assured him. "Such times are times of refreshing. But
the full-time ministry demands many sacrifices." He
pondered a moment, an idea springing from his heart
into his mind. "David, could you possibly come up on
the Sunday afternoon? At Western Vale you're already
halfway there."

David's diary came out of his pocket as if by magic.
"I have an afternoon service only twice in the month."
He flipped the pages eagerly, then sat back and grinned.
"That page is a complete blank."

"I am, of course, asking you for a purpose, David.
On the Sunday morning we shall attend service in the
local church. That will be followed by the Communion
Service. It will, God willing, reach a high spot. We

must endeavour to keep things high until the party breaks up in time for the young folk to get back to Deveringham Road for the evening service. The committee has given a lot of thought to the afternoon programme. They have asked me to choose two young people to speak on 'the call to full-time service'. I had thought of asking Stuart Meredith for one—do you know him, David? You'd like Stuart. He's doing medicine, with a view to going out to the mission field. But now I believe that God has brought *you* here for more than one purpose this afternooon. Stuart is secretary of the house-party—he will be busy with many things, and most of the young folk have already heard his testimony. Will you do this for us, David? No, not for us. For the Lord."

David nodded, too deeply humbled to trust himself to speak. He wondered if he could ever achieve, through God's grace, the wisdom, the understanding, and the spiritual experience of Mr. Cartwright. He found his voice coming from somewhere. "Would you mind telling me who the other speaker will be?" he asked quietly.

Mr. Cartwright frowned very slightly. He loved David dearly. "The other," he said simply, "will be Miss Marguerite Loch."

CHAPTER FIFTEEN

AT four o'clock Julie folded her knitting and put it neatly away. The jumper for poor little Coral was nearing completion. Mrs. Loch had been most kind about the awkward parts and had given Julie advice about the finishing touches before leaving with Marguerite on the previous morning. Julie admired Mrs. Loch intensely. She seemed to know the when and the where and the how of all things. Coral's little jumper looked really nice, and somehow the knitting of it had given comfort in a week which, to Julie, had seemed singularly comfortless.

It was time to make a cup of tea for Miss Loch. Miss Loch was white-haired and gentle, and Julie had liked her at once. She was a lady of independent but small means, and a visit to her nephew's well-appointed home was always a pleasure to her. This time, with Julie to make things comfortable for her (and without Gwendoline to over-organise her) it promised to be more pleasant than ever. Miss Loch, hearing the clink of the spoon in the saucer, told herself that Gwendoline had been more than fortunate in securing Julie's services—it was almost impossible, people said, to get a good girl for the house in these days.

"You do things so nicely, dear," she said appreciatively, as Julie brought the dainty tray to where she sat with her crochet in the sitting-room. "I hope you will have a cup yourself." She would have liked to ask Julie to bring it in with hers, but she wasn't sure of Gwendoline's feelings on such a matter. "Is that a car pulling up at our gate? I expect it will be someone wanting to see my niece. I suppose she is aways in demand."

Julie walked to the window. There *was* a car at the gate. She caught her breath. Not in such cars did people come to visit Mrs. Loch. In this very select neighbourhood it looked even more battered, more disreputable, more antiquated than it had looked at Western Vale. She couldn't fail to recognise Aspidistra, nor the red head of the tall young fellow who was even then halfway up the path. It was the red head of the very last person she wanted to see.

"It *is* a visitor," she said quietly. "I think it is someone to see Marguerite."

David had had some little difficulty in deciding on a pretext for ringing the Loch doorbell. Marguerite had not left her music behind at the church, he had no message for either her or Julie from Mrs. Frost, he had no reasonable request to make. Mr. Cartwright's words had provided him with an excuse. It was a slim one, admittedly, but he told himself that the unenterprising mind, like the faint heart, ne'er won the fair lady. He would ask something about the house-party.

Julie greeted him pleasantly but with even more than her usual reserve. "I expect you've come to see Marguerite," she said.

He hedged. "I just wanted to make an enquiry."

"I'm sorry. She and Mrs. Loch have gone to visit some friends in the country for a week or so."

"Oh." His face betrayed nothing. "I didn't know."

"It was arranged quite suddenly." Julie hesitated, unsure of herself. What would Mrs. Loch wish her to do in such a situation? It was scarcely polite to keep even the rawest of clergymen standing on the doorstep. Mrs. Loch was so passionately correct in things like that. Julie took a chance.

"Would you care to come in, Mr. Sterling? Mr. Loch's aunt is here with me."

It was David's turn to hesitate. Then he, too, took a chance. Mr. Loch's aunt would be an old lady, and he got on well with old ladies. "Thank you," he said. "I'd like to come in."

Miss Loch was delighted. She knew very few young men, and quite certainly she knew none who, in a matter of moments, charmed her into feeling that she was a person of supreme importance in the way that David did. Miss Loch took courage. Gwendoline would never know, and the girl was a lady. "Bring an extra cup for yourself," she whispered to Julie.

Julie was anything but grateful. She said almost nothing. David did his very best, but even he could not break through the shell of reserve which teased and challenged him. She waited on them perfectly, anticipating every small need, knowing precisely what was wanted. David couldn't exactly explain it even to himself, but somehow she reminded him of Mrs. Cartwright, never in the foreground yet always part of it, always behind the one who needed her with a strength and sweetness which never grew less for all the giving, always available, always beloved.

"I expect you miss Marguerite," he said.

"Very much," Julie assured him. No place could be the same without Marguerite's golden presence. She could not tell him that Marguerite's departure had been almost a relief to her. The very thing which should have drawn them most closely together had somehow estranged them, and the thought was unbearable.

"I miss the music," Miss Loch said gently. "Marguerite sings, you know."

David did know. He spoke almost reverently. "She has a very lovely voice." He paused, remembering Hazel, remembering the hush in the bare little church as the words wove themselves into the stillness:

Lord, let the glow of Thy great love
Through my whole being shine.

It was something about which he was loth to speak. He turned his thoughts in another direction.

"Mr. Cartwright was speaking to me about Deveringham Road house-party," he said. "I expect you're looking forward to it."

"Mrs. Loch has given me permission to register for it," Julie said primly. She couldn't very well tell David that she wished now that Mrs. Loch had said 'No'. She *was* looking forward to it, she supposed, but it was with a sense of dread rather than of pleasure. "Marguerite is on the committee, of course," she added hurriedly, anxious to turn attention from herself. "May I take your cup, Mr. Sterling?"

"My name is David," he said.

Julie took Coral's jumper to Western Vale on the following Wednesday. She would have liked to show the finished work to Mrs. Loch, but a cold snap had set in, and the thought of a half-covered Coral was more than Julie could bear. There was another reason for haste which Julie did not like to admit even to herself. This time it would be easier to go to Western Vale without Marguerite.

Hazel was pleased to see her and had much to tell her. She made no secret of her feelings.

"Until Friday," she said, "I felt terrible. Julie, I wished I'd never done it. Stood up in the church, I mean. I didn't disbelieve any of it, mind you. It was just that I thought I'd bitten off more than I could swallow and I'd been fool enough to do it in front of a lot of people. The young fellow came and talked to me on Tuesday; but it didn't make any difference. What he said was all right. I didn't doubt a word of it. It would have been O.K. for other people. Not for *me*, with Andy to cope with. You've no idea how miserable I was, Julie."

Julie was silent. She could have said 'I've been miserable, too, Hazel', but the same force which had glued her to her seat in the Western Vale church held back the words. Hazel, however, waited for no comment.

"On Friday morning Andy reckoned he was crook and would have to stay in bed for the day. He didn't mention the name of his affliction," Hazel said with heavy sarcasm. "He didn't have to. He gets it every time he feels like a day off. In bed he stayed, and who should come to the door but a parson! Not the young

Reverend, but a friend of his. An old man. Mr. Cartwright."

"I know him," Julie breathed.

"He had his wife with him. You know, Julie, she scarcely said a word; yet you could feel her talking through him all the time, if you know what I mean. I knew straight away that I could tell them everything. I didn't know where we could talk, with Andy in the house, and him with ears sticking out like lanterns on a coach, so—Julie, you'll think this is terrible—I shoved some chairs into the laundry and we sat there."

"I don't think it was terrible," Julie whispered. Mr. and Mrs. Cartwright, on the King's business, would fit as royally into a laundry as into anywhere else.

"I made a clean breast of everything. About your father, and you, and marrying Andy, and dragging up the kids like this. I—I can't tell you what they said, Julie. Some of it was the same as what young Sterling said, but it was as if they'd known it a lot longer and they'd found out that there was no catch in it. And then Mr. Cartwright said he'd go in and talk to Andy."

Hazel laughed. "If Andy didn't feel crook before that he certainly felt crook after! Something about the old boy scared him. I still haven't been able to make out what it was. The parson told him just what he thought of him—all in the nicest way, of course—but if Andy had been up and about he'd have knocked him down, and that without any apologies. But, as it was, if he'd got out of bed he'd have proved that he wasn't so sick after all, and Andy's crafty. Anyhow, Mr. Cartwright said he'd come back another day and have a proper talk to him, sort of as if he took pity on even Andy and reckoned he couldn't stand any more in one dose—but he told him one thing straight. We'd have to go without a radiogram until we didn't have to pay for it with proper food and children's shoes and things like that. He said he'd go to the firm himself and see what they would do about it."

Hazel paused, glancing without regret towards the corner where the handsome radiogram had seemed so pitifully out of place. "They came and picked it up this morning," she said. "But to get back to Friday. They talked to me about going to church, and I said I didn't think I could, for two reasons. The man from the grocer's was one of them. He was the fellow giving out the hymnbooks. I didn't see how I could go back to church until I'd paid the bill. Not to hold my head up, I mean. The other thing was the hat. Did you notice it, Julie?"

"I did. It was a lovely hat."

"The young parson got it for me. I don't know where. Andy hadn't seen it then. He'd be furious if he knew. But Mrs. Cartwright said I could quite truthfully tell him that a friend of hers had given it to me. She's known the young parson since he was a boy and she thinks of him just like a son. So I told Andy that, and he took it without a fuss, and I went to church on Sunday night and wore it."

"And the man who gave out the hymnbooks . . .?"

"Mr. Cartwright lent me the money to pay the bill. I fixed it up on Saturday morning."

Julie didn't know what to say. Hazel, who had not disappointed God, was having her needs supplied in a most wonderful way. It seemed an opportune moment for changing the subject and presenting the little jumper for Coral.

Hazel was pleased and touched. "You've got your father's nice ways, Julie," she said. "He never said much but he was always a gentleman. Now Coral'll be able to go to Sunday School."

"Will your—will Mr. Frost mind? Going to Sunday School, I mean."

"He won't want another ear-bashing from the old parson," Hazel said significantly. "I don't say that he'll exactly help me to get them ready, mind you. It'll take more than talking to reform Andy. But the old boy's got him worried, for some reason. He might even have the idea that Mr. Cartwright knows his boss, and it would never do for him to lose his job. It requires less hard work than any other job he's ever heard of. It would not be right," added Hazel, in the hard, tight voice which she reserved for the subject of Andy, "for Mr. Frost to overdo himself."

Julie walked back to the station slowly. There was no special hurry. She had left everything ready for Mr. Loch and his aunt. That had not been strictly necessary, for this was her day off, but it had pleased her to do it. The walk was uninteresting, but her thoughts were busy, and this time she had worn her flatties instead of her best shoes and she would not have been nearly so grateful for a lift in a battered green car as she had been on another occasion. She sighed, scarcely knowing why. If David did happen to come along she'd have nothing to say to him.

Words of Hazel's were imprinting themselves on her mind. She had to admire Hazel. The road ahead presented uncounted difficulties, but Hazel would not turn back now. She had taken her first timorous steps on The Way and with each one she had found God beside her. "Just thinking of you and Marguerite will help me, Julie," she'd said.

Hazel didn't know. She just didn't understand. To Julie it had seemed that everyone in the little church at Western Vale had seen right into her heart, had seen her longing, her hesitancy, her failure. But Hazel hadn't seen anything. . . .

She was glad to get into the train, glad to let its clatter shut out from her fellow-passengers those words which she felt must otherwise be heard by other hearts than her own. "Just thinking of you and Marguerite will help me, Julie."

It wasn't so much Hazel who needed the help. It was Julie herself. She must try to think of something else. Life turned things upside down again so quickly. . . .

CHAPTER SIXTEEN

THE fair white linen cloth which covered the Communion Table had a deep, delicate border of crocheted lace, exquisitely wrought. Julie knew that she had seen that pattern somewhere before. Of course. Miss Loch. Out of nothing but a ball of finest white cotton Miss Loch had created that selfsame fragile tracery of vine-leaves which had, in their turn, reminded Julie of the embossing around the top of the big brass bowl at Roselinden. So many things reminded her of Roselinden, she thought. She was glad about that. For so long Roselinden had been Home.

She was finding it difficult to keep her thoughts in check, to concentrate on what was being said by the special speaker who was the guest of the Christian Endeavour house-party. Somehow she had the feeling that it didn't really matter if she listened or not. What the speaker was saying was so close to what David had said at Western Vale that it almost seemed as if she knew what was coming next. The leaves on the Roselinden bowl had been bigger, but they were the same pretty, pointed shape which had made polishing so difficult. She wondered if Daffodil Baker had improved at all. She thought of Miss Blake, and then of Miss Levering, and then, with the utmost clarity, old Mr. Rose's text swung into her mind.

'My God shall supply all your need according to His riches in glory by Christ Jesus.'

God had done so much for her, but she had disappointed Him. She hadn't been able to get that out of her mind. It seemed too much to expect that He would supply her with a second chance for doing what she should have done in the church at Western Vale.

Miss Loch's vine-leaves had been smaller, of course. She had been making a table mat, not a Communion cloth. Perhaps someone like Miss Loch had crocheted this delicate lace, stitch by stitch. It would have to be someone with plenty of time and lots of patience, someone who wanted to do it for love of Someone else. . . .

Her thoughts flitted to Marguerite. Julie could see her across the church, her expressive face alight and intent. She had come back from her brief visit to the country more glowing than ever, and the house had come alive again with music and sunshine. In Julie's mind there was still a barrier between them; from Marguerite's it had entirely vanished. She was one of those in whom hope springs eternal, and she reasoned that the past was now the past and that the house-party, with all its possibilities, was still to come. She renewed her prayers for Julie.

A certain timid expectancy had somewhat softened the unhappiness in Julie's heart. She had heard a great deal about God since she had arrived with a chattering, cheerful crowd of the young folk from Deveringham Road on the Friday evening. Perhaps God *would* give her a second chance. She tried to get her mind back on what the speaker was saying. 'This is the way, walk ye in it.' It was much the same as what David had said, but the speaker was using longer words and bigger phrases, and he didn't have David's nice smile. She had a fleeting impression of David's hand in hers, leading her to Christ Who was the Way, and the Truth, and the Life, slipping her timorous hand out of his and into a stronger, firmer One. Perhaps the speaker might even do what David had done as he closed his address. God might even give her the other chance on this very morning, in this quite beautiful mountain-side church where the local congregation had joined with the young folk of the house-party. He might.

The sermon was coming to an end. A note of appeal warmed the speaker's voice. Julie waited, tense and ready. The words that were spoken seemed of no un-usual significance. They simply pointed the people to Jesus Christ, just as David had done. She had already put her hand into His. She didn't have to do that again. What she did have to do was to acknowledge Him.

The speaker paused. This is it, Julie told herself. She put her feet into the right position. She was going to be ready to stand this time. She didn't want to be shuffling her feet, spoiling in even the smallest degree the sanctity of the moment for which she was waiting. At Western Vale it had seemed too hard; here, strangely enough, it seemed almost too easy.

The voice of the speaker came again, clear and pene-trating. He repeated his text. 'This is the way, walk ye in it.' He paused again.

"Amen," he said.

They had almost finished singing the closing hymn by the time Julie's numbed senses awakened to full realisation. She had been wrong, after all. God wasn't going to give her a second chance. It *had* been too much to expect. The wretchedness which had filled her heart at Western Vale was as nothing to that which overwhelmed her now.

She stood with bowed head, awaiting the Benediction. All she wanted to do was to get outside. The Communion Service was to follow, but she could have no part in that. Had things worked out differently she believed that she would have been entitled to go forward to the Communion rail. But she couldn't do that *now*. People would think that she just didn't understand the meaning of what she was doing. When the Benediction was over she would slip quietly out, as she'd done on the occasions when the Communion Table had been spread at Deveringham Road. No-one, now, would expect her to do anything else.

It was Mr. Cartwright's voice which came through the stillness.

"Following the Benediction," he said quietly, "the Sacrament of the Lord's Supper will be administered. Please do not leave the church unless you have responsibilities elsewhere. If you do not desire to partake of the Communion itself, you may still share in the blessing by remaining prayerfully in your seat. To all those who believe in and love the Lord Jesus Christ, to all who seek to follow and serve Him, I offer a loving invitation to meet with us around His Table, in remembrance of what He has done for us."

That's me, Julie thought. No-one but Mr. Cartwright could have put it all into such simple, beautiful words. I do believe in Him. I do love Him. I do want to follow and serve Him. But no-one knows that. . . .

Helen Spencer quietly opened the little book in which the order of service was printed and held it out for Julie to share. It was nice of her to do that, Julie thought, with her own special friend Bill Meredith sitting without a book at the end of the seat. She liked Helen best of all the girls. Next to Marguerite, of course. Marguerite was different from everyone else. It was nice, too, that it was Mr. Cartwright who was going to conduct the Communion service. It seemed more homely like that. I'll watch the words in the book, Julie told herself. That's all I *can* do.

Out of the corner of her eye she saw again the vine-leaf pattern of the Communion cloth. Miss Loch's table mat had been of the same delicate daintiness. Julie's mind pictured it again, lying on the broad arm of Miss Loch's chair while Miss Loch sipped her cup of tea and talked to David. She had felt uncomfortable enough then, Julie remembered. She felt a thousand times more uncomfortable now. . . .

The words of the service were new to her. Julie kept her eyes on the book. Mr. Cartwright's voice was fraught with love and tenderness. "We do not presume to come to this Thy Table, O merciful Lord, trusting in our own righteousness, but in Thy manifold and great mercies . . ." Could she dare go forward? Even as she asked herself the question Julie knew that she couldn't.

Suddenly she realised that Mr. Cartwright was saying something that wasn't in the book. She looked up. He was standing behind the Communion rail, his old face lit with the understanding of years, his whole soul reaching out to those who sat motionless in the church.

"Perhaps," he said, "there are those among us this morning who have never before partaken of the Holy Communion. Perhaps it is something that you have wanted to do for some time. It may even be that during this morning's service you have, for the first time, felt your need of a closer communion with the Lord Jesus Christ." He paused, and there was no word which could have described the way in which his soul was reflected in his smile. "If so, will you please come forward first?"

Julie never had more than the haziest recollection of getting to her feet, of passing Helen and Bill, of walking up the aisle. She only knew that she was at the Communion rail, kneeling, with Mr. Cartwright standing before her, a chased silver plate in his hand. There were two others kneeling beside her, but she did not see them. She did not even consciously see Mr. Cartwright. She saw only the Cross, and Jesus Christ Who had died for her, that He might bring her to God—to God, Who had supplied all her needs; to God Who, in a way too simple, too wonderful for words, had given her a second chance. . . .

She heard God's voice speaking to her. "The Body of our Lord Jesus Christ, which was given for thee, preserve thee unto everlasting life. Take and eat this in remembrance that Christ died for thee . . ."

It was Mr. Cartwright's voice, of course, but it was God Who was speaking through him. She had known that the organ was playing softly. Now she recognised the tune. It was the old Roselinden favourite. She knew every word of every verse.

> *He died that we might be forgiven,*
> *He died to make us good,*
> *That we might go at last to Heaven,*
> *Saved by His precious blood.*

Mr. Cartwright was standing before her again. "The Blood of our Lord Jesus Christ, which was shed for thee, preserve thee unto everlasting life. Drink this in remembrance that Christ's blood was shed for thee . . ."

Julie set down the cup. The service had been so simple, so orderly, that she had known what to do without being told. For one moment she lifted her head and looked into the face of Mr. Cartwright, sharing with him the happiness, the absolute trust, which was in her heart. Then she bowed her head again. She was conscious that Mr. Cartwright's arms were uplifted as if in bestowal of a blessing.

"Go in peace," he said.

CHAPTER SEVENTEEN

IT was cold on the mountainside, but Julie didn't mind. There were cheery log fires in the sprawling, comfortable old house which the Deveringham Road young folk had used more than once for a house-party; there was bustle and laughter and the harmonious sound of the Christian Endeavour choir practising their anthem for the evening service; but Julie was drawn by none of these. More than anything else she wanted to get away by herself for a few minutes before the 'bus came, in an hour or so, to take the young people back to Deveringham Road. She wanted quietness, solitude, the opportunity to seal within herself all the wonderful things which now were hers. She pulled her warm coat closely around her, wrapping herself into a world of her own, and slipped noiselessly away through the trees to a secluded little spot which overlooked the deep valleys of the stately Blue Mountains.

Everything was packed and ready to go, her own things and Marguerite's. The afternoon meeting was over. The words of both Marguerite and David had made a tremendous impression. Julie had never been more proud of Marguerite. She had only wished that she herself had more to give to the Lord, but Julie knew her own limitations. At present she could do nothing more than give satisfaction to Mrs. Loch, and perhaps the Lord might give her some bigger work for Him later on.

She found a comfortable-looking log and sat down on it. She was still within sight and sound of the house —she could hear Marguerite's voice, taking the solo part in the anthem—but it was as though she had come away into a world of her own. She almost resented it when she heard footsteps on the path behind her, and, turning, she saw that it was David who was coming.

He sat on the log beside her.

"Marguerite told me," he said.

She nodded, knowing what it was that he meant. She herself had had no conversation with him since his arrival early in the afternoon. He had nodded and smiled at her from a distance, but to Marguerite he had talked and to Marguerite he had listened. Julie had heard someone say that they would make a lovely couple.

"I'm glad," she whispered. There was so much more that she wanted to say. She wanted to tell him what had happened at Western Vale. But the right words did not come.

He was silent for a moment. He seemed to understand. "You don't say very much, do you, Julie?"

"I think a lot," she said shyly.

David frowned. "I expect that I sometimes say too much."

"I liked what you said this afternoon," Julie said, greatly daring. She added, surprised at her own temerity: "I wish I had more to give Him."

"You've given Him yourself, Julie. That's everything."

"There seems so little of me to give. Marguerite has so much. I——" She looked down at her hands, their fingers intertwined on her lap. She held them up. "They're all I have to give."

"And you've given them, Julie?"

She nodded. "This afternoon."

"Sorry to interrupt," said Stuart Meredith's quiet voice, "but there's an urgent 'phone message for you, David. One of your church folk has had to be taken to hospital and the neighbours think you might be able to arrange something about the children. No-one seems to know where the father is."

David was on his feet in an instant. Julie liked him for that. He had meant what he said about giving God everything.

"Does Mr. Cartwright know?" he asked.

"Yes. He took the message. He says that if you leave immediately you may be able to do something before your evening service. The name, by the way, is Frost."

Mrs. Loch replaced the telephone, wrote something more on the pad which was already almost covered with notes, and rose to her feet, satisfied. Once again she, Mrs. Philip Loch, had pulled all the right strings and had achieved the impossible. She went in search of Julie.

Julie was arranging chrysanthemums in a wide green bowl. She was doing it as she did everything else, with neatness and precision and real grace; but her mind was far from her hands, and with it she was endeavouring to climb over obstacles which seemed altogether insurmountable. She looked at the clock. Five minutes to ten. It was difficult to believe that, twenty-four hours earlier, she had been at the sprawling old house on the mountainside and all the tremendous experiences of the day still lay before her. Mrs. Loch's crisp voice almost startled her.

"Everything has been arranged, Julie. The Boy's Home I mentioned will be pleased to take Timothy. Miss Levering raised difficulties about the little girl. She said that there was already a waiting-list at Rose-linden. I could not accept *that*. I have spoken to the Chairman of Directors and he has everything in hand. There will be a bed for—Coral, is it?—to-morrow. At Cottage Two. I specified that. I have also spoken to the hospital. Mrs. Frost is resting comfortably, and there is no need for alarm. I have also spoken to Mr.——" Mrs. Loch consulted the pad in her hand— "yes, to Mr. Sterling. He will meet you at Western Vale station at two o'clock and will take you to Mrs. Frost's home. You will collect and pack the children's personal belongings. There is probably very little. One of the neighbours is washing the clothes they had on yesterday, and another has taken charge of the children for a night or two. There is also news of the whereabouts of Mr. Frost."

"Where is he?" Julie breathed.

"He is, I regret to say, being detained by the police. I understand that this is not the first occasion. He was arrested on Saturday evening for drunk and disorderly conduct."

A lump which impeded speech came into Julie's throat. Poor Hazel. She slipped her hand into her apron pocket and took out her handkerchief.

"These things are sometimes all for the best," said Mrs. Loch briskly. She disliked tears. "It is evident that this man needs to be brought to his senses. It will be necessary for us to have an early lunch, Julie. I am then quite prepared for you to take the rest of the day off so that you can endeavour to do something for these poor unfortunate children."

"Thank you, Mrs. Loch," Julie said faintly. She added shyly: "You are very kind." Mrs. Loch, to whom Hazel and her children would have been socially quite unacceptable, was surely going the second mile on their behalf in the name of organised charity. There seemed no limit to what Mrs. Loch could do when such an occasion arose.

David was waiting at Western Vale station. Aspidistra looked surprisingly clean and bright. It was as well that neither Julie nor David could hear Mrs. Featherberry's comments on the minister who could stay outside polishing his car and whistling 'To God be the glory' after she had called him to lunch *three* times.

He turned the innocent Aspidistra in the direction of Crossley Road.

"I thought Marguerite might have come with you," he said casually.

"She wanted to," Julie assured him. "Mrs. Loch——" She pulled herself up quickly. Mrs. Loch had made it

F

quite clear that for Julie to come into intimate contact
with the Frost household was one thing, for Marguerite another. "Mrs. Loch wanted her to go somewhere
else," she finished lamely.

He did not comment. He smiled to himself. It was so
very evident that Julie, like everyone else, had jumped
to the obvious but the wrong conclusion. He told her
what he knew of Hazel and the children. Mrs. McGlynn,
it seemed, had risen to the occasion very well indeed.
She had gone with Hazel in the ambulance, and Mrs.
Brown from the farm across the road had offered to
take the children for a night or two. People were kind
when you got to know them, David said.

"And Hazel?" Julie enquired anxiously. "Did Mrs.
McGlynn——?"

"I don't really know what happened, Julie," he said
gently. "Somehow she let Mrs. McGlynn know that she
was ill. The doctor says she will be in hospital—or
possibly a sanatorium—for three, four, perhaps six
months. They're still not sure of what the trouble is.
She hadn't had any medical attention for years—the
doctor said she hadn't even been having proper food
for a long time . . ."

They were both silent, shocked at the sharp realisation of something that could happen at their very
doors to someone for whom both had a sincere affection. Then Julie spoke.

"Mr. Frost? Will he be—away—long?"

David shook his head. "Only a few days, I think.
Mr. Cartwright has been in touch with the police. God
moves in a mysterious way, Julie. Mr. Cartwright hap-

CHAPTER EIGHTEEN

ɪᴛ had been arranged that the Frost children would leave Western Vale with Mrs. McGlynn and that Mrs. Loch would meet them on a certain train and, from that point, take charge of Coral. Things, however, did not work out exactly as planned. For once, Mrs. Loch found that she had met her match, in the shape of an influenza germ that was stronger even than the will of Mrs. Philip Loch, and she had to accept the fact that, for a day or two at least, all organising would have to be done from her bed.

"It will be necessary for you to take the child to Roselinden, Julie," she said. "I have already given Miss Levering all details. I would not like to think that anything has been overlooked just because I am unable to attend to it myself."

"We'll see to everything, Mummy," Marguerite assured her. "Don't worry about a single thing." She was perched on the side of her mother's bed, watching Julie as she deftly did the very few things that were necessary to set the patient's room in perfect order. "I'll go with Julie and we'll fix everything up just as you'd do it yourself. Won't we, Julie?"

It would have been a bold influenza germ that caused Mrs. Loch to agree to that. "Julie should not be away more than an hour or so," she pointed out. "I shall

be glad to have someone with me in the house durin
that time, Marguerite."

Marguerite was thoroughly disappointed. Th
thought of taking the neglected little Coral Frost t
her new and beautiful home at Roselinden made
strong appeal to her. Her feet had never quite touche
the earth since her return on the Sunday night from a
the high experiences of the mountainside; she coul
still feel the exaltation of that moment when Julie ha
gone forward to the Communion rail, she could sti
catch the vision which had shone before her as sh
had spoken from her heart to all the young folk on th
Sunday afternoon; even in the unfolding of this ne
chapter in the story of Hazel she saw God's hand ver
clearly. And all these things, she realised suddenly, ha
some bearing on her desire to go to Roselinden wit
Julie and Coral. . . .

She had challenged even herself when she had tol
the others of her call to full-time service for the Lord
Never had her desire to serve Him been more urgen
more intense; and she had faced up to herself wit
absolute sincerity. Was it possible that God did no
really want her to be a deaconess, or to go into Bibl
College? Going in for things like that took time. Coul
it be that He had some other work for her, work tha
was close at hand, work in which she was needed im
mediately? There was but one thing for her to do. Sh
must keep herself alert and ready for His guid
ance.

She was at the piano when Julie returned from Rose
linden. Mrs. Loch was restlessly asleep. There wa

nothing that Marguerite could do for her. She heard
Julie come in and she called to her, her fingers still
softly caressing the keys and calling forth the signifi-
cant strains of her beloved 'Westminster New'. Almost under her breath she sang one verse of it as Julie
sank wearily into a chair.

> *Make this poor self grow less and less,*
> *Be Thou my life and aim;*
> *Oh, make me daily, through Thy grace,*
> *More meet to bear Thy name.*

She turned to Julie.

"Tell me all about it," she invited.

"There isn't much to tell," Julie said. It had all been
rather a strain, so far as she was concerned. Going to
her new home at Roselinden had been viewed anything
but gratefully by young Coral, and she had been terri-
fied by the vastness and cleanliness of the place and
especially by Miss Levering. It was going to take time
for Coral to settle in. Some children were like that,
Julie remembered. "Coral wasn't very happy about
it all," she admitted.

"Poor little soul." In a moment of insight Marguerite
saw it all. The child would be so pathetically alone.
"Did you remember everything that Mummy told you,
Julie?"

"I hope so," Julie said soberly. Miss Levering hadn't
been quite her usual gracious self. Julie knew why that
was. She resented Mrs. Loch's over-ruling of her
authority in the matter of Coral Frost. Miss Levering
had been ready for them on arrival. There had been

no waiting on the long seat with the carved ends this time. It was only as she left Miss Levering's office that Julie lingered to re-read every faded word of old Mr. Rose's text. She understood it all now. It took her mind so completely back to the indescribable experiences of the mountainside that she did not even think to observe Daffodil Baker's progress with the big brass bowl.

"And how is my friend Miss Blake?" Marguerite enquired. "I must go to see Miss Blake again one day."

"She's worn out," said Julie briefly. She was worried about Miss Blake. She couldn't keep going, year after year, like this. The young woman with the dangling ear-rings had gone the way of all the others. Most of the time Miss Blake was doing the work of two. Julie got up.

"I saw some nice fresh oranges in the shop on the corner," she said. "I'll go and squeeze some for your mother."

Marguerite went to Roselinden two days later.

She did not go without considerable thought. It was not what she wanted to do, but she had talked it over with the Lord many times and it had been made quite plain to her that the only thing which stood in her way was Marguerite Loch herself. She had not mentioned her decision to anyone. That, perhaps, had been foolish, she admitted to herself; but for the present it was a matter that lay between Marguerite Loch and her Lord.

She thought of Julie as she walked the pleasant tree-lined mile. She was very happy about Julie. Her prayers had been answered. It did not seem to matter now that Julie had no people of her own. Julie had everything else that counted, and she was beginning to make friends. Helen Spencer had told Marguerite that she liked Julie very much. That was good. Helen was a nice girl. The stately gates of Roselinden came into view as Marguerite turned the corner.

She had made no appointment, but Miss Levering, she found, was willing to see her. She took the chair which had, more than once, been occupied by Julie herself. She smiled at Miss Levering.

"I am Marguerite Loch," she said steadily. She added, with a note of justifiable pride in her voice: "My mother is a member of the Roselinden committee."

Miss Levering was not a woman to harbour grudges. Generally speaking she was not one who permitted herself to have any feelings at all. Feelings interfered with efficiency, and efficiency must come first in all things. But Mrs. Loch had done something inexcusable. . . .

"I am aware of that," she said stiffly.

She looked at the girl who sat across from her, her young face alight with eagerness and purpose. She had heard that Mrs. Loch's daughter was a beautiful girl. It was true enough. There was no trace of encouragement in her voice when she spoke.

"Is there something I can do to help you?"

"Perhaps *I* can help *you*," Marguerite said softly. This was the moment, the moment of self-forgetfulness. She had been slow to recognise God's Will for her, but now there was no mistake about it. "I have come to offer my services to Roselinden."

"In what capacity?" asked Miss Levering crisply.

For a moment Marguerite was nonplussed. She supposed that there must be some name for those who served under the banner of Miss Blake, but she doubted if she had ever heard it. "That would be for you to say," she said diplomatically.

"Have you come in answer to an advertisement, Miss Loch?"

"Oh no." God didn't advertise in the papers. He spoke to the heart. "I believe it is what the Lord wants me to do," she said simply.

Miss Levering was momentarily taken aback. People gave all sorts of reasons for wanting to be employed by Roselinden. There had been many who had said they had been called to the work, but no-one had spoken with the frankness and simplicity of this girl. Miss Levering was embarrassed. To speak of the Almighty in so familiar a way was, she felt, almost indelicate. She met candour with candour.

"What are your qualifications?" she asked bluntly.

"I love children, Miss Levering. They like *me* too. I was leader of the I.S.C.F. at High School, and I have a dear little Sunday School class at Deveringham Road."

Miss Levering was interested in neither the I.S.C.F. nor Deveringham Road. "A love of children is very desirable in work of this nature, Miss Loch, but it could scarcely be called a qualification. The care of children has many aspects. Can you sew?"

"Oh yes." Sewing on C. Miller's buttons had been rather fun. Involuntarily she looked down at her trim grey suit, glad that it covered the buttonless spot on her nylon blouse.

"And darn? School socks, stockings . . ."

"I darned my own school stockings for years," Marguerite assured her. Her mother had said that you couldn't exactly call it *darning*, but Miss Blake would show her how to do it properly. She smiled disarmingly. "They were black. I hated them."

Miss Levering had time for neither smiles nor digressions. "Have you a good basic knowledge of housekeeping? The girls do most of the actual work, of course, but it is essential that the person in charge should know how to direct them."

"I haven't had a *lot* of experience," Marguerite said cautiously. She would have to get Julie to coach her. Julie would know all about it. The vocational guidance officers at school had told the teachers that Marguerite Loch had the ability to learn anything if she put her mind to it. She couldn't quote that to Miss Levering; but she did feel that she could give herself one shred of commendation. "I learn quickly, Miss Levering."

"Are you a good cook?"

This was a surprise. "I thought . . ." Marguerite faltered.

"An assistant is required to undertake the cooking when the Cottage cook is off duty, or in an emergency, Miss Loch."

"I haven't had *much* experience . . ." She had learned how to cook eggs in three ways, on camping holidays, and she had a fair idea as to what went into ice-cream. That was a start. Even Julie hadn't known everything about cooking and Mrs. Loch was still training her. With God nothing was impossible. "I expect I just need some practice," she said optimistically.

"Have you had much to do with under-privileged children?"

"Oh yes." Timmy and Coral were surely as under-privileged as any children could be, and there were two little girls in her Sunday School class who had a shabby look about them.

"The hours are long, Miss Loch. Very long. The conditions are good, but they are extremely exacting."

"I don't mind how hard it is," Marguerite breathed. She had told the Lord that, and she knew that she would not do it in her own strength. She wished that Miss Levering would unbend a little, but she supposed that it was necessary for her to be very cautious and no doubt she was just going through a routine. Her mother had always spoken in the highest terms of Miss Levering's efficiency.

Miss Levering took a book from the drawer of her desk. "I will enter the particulars relating to your— application, Miss Loch. Your name is——?"

"Marguerite."

"Your address?"

"Forty-four Barraclough Avenue."

"Of course." Miss Levering paused. There was something about this girl with the light of a mission in her eyes. The children would adore her. For one moment Miss Levering's purpose wavered. Then she took up the knife which was to cut Marguerite Loch to the quick. One clean, swift wound was all that was needed.

"And your age, Miss Loch?"

"I shall be eighteen in October," Marguerite said with dignity.

Miss Levering put her pen down.

"I am afraid our discussion has been pointless," she said. There was no shade of expression on her face. "The directors are adamant on one point. Roselinden employs no person who is under the age of twenty-one years."

Through the sickness of disappointment and bewilderment which enveloped her, Marguerite was conscious of one stabbing realisation. Miss Levering had known all along that she was too young. She had set out, purposely, to humiliate her. Such a thing had never before happened to Marguerite Loch. She rose to her feet, and something of her mother's pride came to her aid and helped her to keep the tears from her voice though not from her eyes. It was absurd, Miss Levering thought, but she could almost fancy that the girl was wearing her mother's fur cape. . . .

"I think," Marguerite said steadily, "that it would have been better for us both if you had mentioned that to begin with. Good afternoon, Miss Levering."

It took Miss Levering all of five minutes to settle back to her work. The girl had her mother's spirit. She also had something else which Miss Levering couldn't identify, and it was that something which had been hurt. She felt as if she had taken a priceless, fragile piece of china and dashed it in pieces on the floor.

At the majestic gates of Roselinden Marguerite paused, looking back towards Cottage Two. She had meant to call on Miss Blake and to enquire for Coral, but she could not do that now. There was only one person to whom she could talk in this overwhelming moment, and to talk to someone she must. She turned her feet in the right direction.

CHAPTER NINETEEN

MR. CARTWRIGHT was at home. He was helpfulness itself; and one thing led to another. Over a cup of tea, and thickly-buttered slices of Mrs. Cartwright's special sultana loaf, Marguerite told him not only of her experience at Roselinden but of many, many other things. The whole problem of her future she lay before him.

"I don't want to go to the University," she said stubbornly. "I want to serve the Lord *now*. It would waste *years*, Mr. Cartwright. Christ put no special emphasis on learning. The disciples weren't good scholars. They just loved Him and gave Him their best."

He had heard this before, many times. To him it was no new thought, no surprising revelation. In his long ministry he had met with it on countless occasions. Young people were in a hurry—always.

"Those who have gained much can give much," he said quietly. "Christ Himself knew that He wanted to be about His Father's business when He was just twelve years of age. He did not begin His active ministry until He was thirty. The years between were not wasted, Marguerite. They were years of training, of preparation——"

"He didn't go to the University and take a degree so that He could have letters after His name——"

"He did what He believed to be His Father's Will for Him."

Marguerite sighed impatiently. "I cannot see that it is God's Will that I should go to the University for years when I could prepare myself for service in some other way. There *are* other ways, Mr. Cartwright."

He took his Bible and turned to the end of the second chapter of St. Luke's Gospel. " 'And He went down with them'," he read, " 'and came to Nazareth, and was subject unto them . . .' "

He looked at Marguerite and smiled affectionately. "They were His parents, lassie. The parents that God had chosen for Him. He was so right in everything He did."

She had no answer for that. He went on, quietly. "The mission field is crying out for school teachers, Marguerite. A teacher of any standing is of tremendous value to the Lord. A teacher with a degree is of far greater value in many fields."

"I'm not sure that I'd like to be a teacher."

"You might consider pharmacy. Or medicine." He turned and put fresh wood on the cheery little fire. "Doctor Stuart Meredith will have unparalleled opportunities for serving the Lord in the years to come."

She pouted. "Those are difficult courses."

"Not too difficult for Marguerite Loch and the Lord."

"They'd cost a lot of money."

He smiled. "Not more than Marguerite Loch's father could afford to pay."

"I almost believe that you've been talking to Mummy," she said suspiciously.

He shook his head. "I have never spoken to your mother," he reminded her quietly. He sat silent for a moment, looking into the fire. She slipped from her seat and curled up on the mat at his feet, holding out her pretty hands to the warmth. The question he asked seemed almost irrelevant. "How old were you when you gave your heart to the Lord, lassie?"

"I was fourteen. You remember——"

"I remember very well. You were so sure. Sometimes one wonders. There was never any doubt in my mind about *you*, Marguerite."

"There was never any doubt in my own mind," she whispered. "Why have you asked me this?"

"Let's put it this way. There are three Ds which are the three steps to Discipleship. The first is Decision. We've just spoken of that. There were no doubts in your mind when you were fourteen. There are no doubts now?"

She shook her head. The old light was in her face.

"I could never doubt His love for me," she said simply.

"The second D is Dedication. It takes us a step farther. It comes when we are prepared to give Him not only our hearts but our whole selves. It sometimes takes us a long time to reach that second step. You have reached it, lassie. I have never doubted that, either. I was more sure than ever when I listened to you on Sunday afternoon. Your words—and David's—seemed to come from the Lord Himself."

He was silent again. "And the third D?" she prompted.

He smiled. "Can you guess?"

"Determination?" she hazarded.

He put his old hand on her honey-gold curls. "That's a very useful thing for a disciple to have, Marguerite. The D I really mean is a harder one to accept. We rebel against it, most of us. It's Discipline."

She pulled a face, yet somehow she felt better within herself now that so many things had been put into words. "I see what you mean," she said slowly. Then she laughed up at him. "There wouldn't be a piece of sultana loaf left on the plate, would there?"

He handed the plate to her. "Two pieces." There were still some things that must be said, but it would be easier to say them now. "Has anyone ever told you, Marguerite, that you are a very dear lassie?"

"No-one as nice as you," she said prettily.

"You and David are friends, aren't you?"

"Of course. Good friends."

"Special friends?"

She was busy cleaning the crumbs from her fingers. It was a job that called for much concentration. "Not exactly. Not—yet."

He looked at her, curled companionably at his feet. He had never had a daughter of his own. He did not want to hurt her, but he loved her. "Keep things as they are, Marguerite," he said earnestly. "Anything else wouldn't work out. You're too much alike, you and David. A bright colour needs a subdued background if it is to be fully effective." He paused. "I love you both, lassie. That's why I say it."

She knew that she must either laugh or cry. The sound which came was a brave blending of both.

"Discipline?" she queried in a voice which sounded unlike her own.

He nodded. "Discipline," he said.

She uncurled herself and rose to her feet. "It's been quite an afternoon," she commented. "I've learned such a lot of things about myself!"

Her tone was light, but it did not deceive him. Marguerite Loch was an intelligent girl, and deep down she was pure gold. "May I tell you one thing more?" he asked.

She laughed resignedly. "One more can't make a lot of difference!"

" 'The king's daughter is all glorious within; her clothing is of wrought gold,' " he quoted. "Those are shining words, Marguerite. Yet I never see them as the Psalmist meant me to see them. I see them as a picture of you; the glow within, the glow without."

He patted her on the shoulder. "It's true, Marguerite. You *are* the King's daughter. With a capital K."

A sudden thought appealed to her. "So is Julie—now."

"So is Julie." He smiled tenderly, remembering. "I wish you could have seen her face as she knelt at the Communion rail on Sunday morning. Was it only last Sunday morning, Marguerite? So much seems to have happened . . . There was one special moment when it almost seemed to my foolish old eyes that she looked like *you* . . ."

Marguerite walked home slowly. The day was drawing to a close, and the cars and the 'buses and the pedestrians were all homeward bound and it seemed that everyone but she was hurrying. She was so completely oblivious to all that was going on around her that she almost stepped off the footpath in front of an oncoming 'bus that was crowded with suddenly startled passengers. She stepped back quickly, shocked and embarrassed. The road cleared, and she crossed in safety as the 'bus pulled up at the next corner to set down a little group of passengers. All but a tall young fellow with a brief-case had disappeared by the time Marguerite herself reached the corner.

"Stuart!" she said, and there was something in her voice which almost made him believe that she was glad to see him. "I didn't know that this was your stop," she added ingenuously.

He smiled. "It isn't. I just thought that it looked as if you needed someone to look after you."

The simple words somehow brought balm to her wounded spirit. "I think that's just what I do need," she acknowledged soberly.

He left her at her own gate. They had not talked of anything in particular. It was better that way, Marguerite told herself. Her own thoughts needed so much sorting-out that they were best left unexpressed. She stood for a moment and watched him as he walked away, his smooth dark head held high. She wondered why she had always more or less bracketed him in her mind with Underwood Stacey. They were as different as chalk and cheese. Stuart had character. He was nice-looking, too. It was a curious thing that she had never noticed that before. . . .

Doctor Stuart Meredith. She'd never thought of him as that, either. . . .

Her mother was in the sitting-room, the influenza germ having been sufficiently conquered to permit of her coming downstairs in her dressing-gown to sit at the fireside. In the muted, rosy light which came from a standard lamp Marguerite looked at her home. It seemed, suddenly, to hold out to her welcoming arms. She crossed to her mother's side. Her mother looked better, brighter. It was clear that something had pleased her.

"I did intend to go and see Miss Blake and Coral," Marguerite said with perfect truth. "I went to see Mr. Cartwright instead."

Mrs. Loch made no comment. She smiled significantly. "I had a visitor, too," she said. "The Reverend Mr. Sterling."

Marguerite perched herself on the arm of her mother's chair and eased off her shoes. She spoke guardedly. "That was nice, Mummy."

"He came to bring some messages for Julie from Mrs. Frost. I have promised that Julie will go to visit her on Saturday afternoon. I should be quite well enough to spare her by that time. Mr. Sterling stayed for afternoon tea with me."

"That was nice," Marguerite repeated.

"A very charming young man," Mrs. Loch pronounced approvingly. "And a thorough gentleman. His attitude to Julie was most courteous. I accepted that as a personal compliment. Julie has blossomed amazingly since she came to live with us. I was sorry that you were not at home, my dear. You will be interested to know that Mr. Sterling and I discovered that we were already acquainted."

Marguerite was not only interested but greatly surprised. "You'd met David, Mummy? Where?"

Mrs. Loch smiled the smile of one who proposes to keep a tantalising secret. "At St. Cuthbert's."

"But——" That couldn't be right. David himself had said, on the day of his first meeting with Marguerite, that he didn't even know where St. Cuthbert's was. She couldn't very well tell her mother that. Her mother never made a mistake. She lapsed into silence.

"I have invited him to call again at any time," Mrs. Loch went on. She gave her daughter a sidelong glance, but Marguerite was intently looking into the heart of the fire. "He seemed most happy to accept the invitation," she added pointedly.

"I see," said Marguerite slowly. It was a pity that such visits were going to be wasted. Commonsense already told her that Mr. Cartwright was right, and after all she had always preferred dark hair to red. She turned the conversation into another channel. "I've been thinking, Mummy. The year is slipping away, isn't it? Could we have a little talk about what I'm going to do?"

She felt her mother stiffen beside her. "You've been talking to Mr. Cartwright about this, Marguerite?"

"Yes."

"Must you always talk things over with other people before you talk them over with me?"

There was no answer for that. If she had taken her mother into her confidence she would have been spared bitter humiliation at the hands of Miss Levering. And yet—God had used that very thing to bring her face to face with herself . . . Some day she believed that she would be able to tell her mother all about it. . . .

She felt suddenly closer to her mother. Discipline, Mr. Cartwright had said. It was a curious thing that, all at once, it seemed easy to say the words that she had to say.

She slipped from the arm of her mother's chair and coiled herself into another on the other side of the fireplace. She wanted to watch the pleasure, the satisfaction, come into her mother's face.

"Do you think that Daddy could afford to put me through pharmacy?" she asked quietly. "Or medicine?"

CHAPTER TWENTY

THE REVEREND DAVID STERLING whistled merrily as
he polished the shoes on his feet and kept the corner
of his eye on the door lest the disapproving Mrs.
Featherberry might appear. A truly brilliant inspiration had come to him and he had turned a more than
ready ear to its persuasion. On this sunny Saturday
afternoon he would go again to the hospital and visit
Mrs. Frost.

Even as he whistled he was conscious of Mrs.
Featherberry's approach. She stood in the doorway,
watching him. He put a final shine on the toe of his
right shoe before he bestowed on her an impudent and
wholly affectionate grin.

"Copped!" he said cheerfully.

"A Reverend should set a good example," she reminded him, in a tone which implied that she had said
this countless times before and would continue to say
it until the end. "And you all dressed up in your best
suit! If you had a hat I've no doubt you'd have *that*
on, too. I thought you were going to stay at home
and do something to your car this afternoon."

"That *was* my intention," David conceded. "I think
now that it might hang together until after Sunday.
Mrs. Featherberry, I have a very strong feeling that I
should visit Mrs. Frost again this afternoon."

"It's only two days since you went," Mrs. Featherberry said bluntly. "You haven't heard that she's worse, have you?" she asked suddenly.

"Oh no. It's just—It's like this, Mrs. F. She hasn't many friends, you know. She won't have a lot of people to see her. It's nice to have visitors when you're in hospital, isn't it?"

Mrs. Featherberry softened. It wasn't every young man who'd give up his Saturday afternoon for the sake of a poor soul like the woman from Crossley Road. She cast around in her mind for some way of equalling his self-sacrifice.

"If I'd known that you were going I'd have made a cake for you to take," she said magnanimously.

It was David's turn to be impressed. The Guild ladies were inclined to say that Mrs. Featherberry was rather sparing with her giving, and David knew that, even in sickness, Mrs. Featherberry held a very poor opinion of the good Mrs. McGlynn's neighbour. "Mrs. Frost would have appreciated that," he said sincerely.

Mrs. Featherberry pondered. "There's the apple tart I made for your tea to-night, Reverend Sterling. The poor thing might fancy a bit of something home-made, do you think? You'd have to come home to bread and jam yourself——"

"I *love* bread and jam," David said firmly. He probably wouldn't even notice what he was eating when it came to tea-time. Unless Mrs. Featherberry changed her mind, of course. . . .

Mrs. Featherberry watched him rattle off down the road. He had a long way to go in a car that might only just hang together until after Sunday. She was proud of him. She looked at the clock.

It was time for her afternoon nap, but she knew that she wouldn't rest while she had bread and jam on her conscience. The young Reverend would be sure to come home hungry. She opened the cupboard and took out the mixing-bowl.

At the turn in the hospital stairs Julie paused. She was neither upstairs nor down, and she was alone. Her mind went back over the months. She thought of her first day at Mrs. Loch's, of old Mr. Rose's text, of Marguerite waiting for her with the brown hat held on the honey-gold curls. Julie corrected herself. Things were so different now. She was neither upstairs nor down, but she was not alone.

She moved on. Hazel would be thinking that she wasn't coming. It wasn't likely that she'd have any other visitors on this sunny Saturday afternoon. At the top of the stairs Julie hesitated. David had told her that she would find Hazel in the ward on the left. In the second bed from the door, David had said. That was simple enough. She was about to move towards the door when she heard someone coming up the stairs behind her, coming quickly yet quietly, taking the last three steps as one; and suddenly she felt a hand slip into hers and, turning, she saw David.

"Julie," he said.

She had no words for him. Fleetingly she dared to look into his eyes, and she knew that Marguerite's prayers had all been answered. God, Who had supplied her every need, had also found for Julie Westaway someone who belonged to her. For one moment she let her hand linger in David's; then she smiled demurely.

"I expect you've come to see Hazel," she said.

"With an apple tart from Mrs. Featherberry's own hand!" he assured her solemnly. Then he laughed. "Julie, do you think that Mrs. Frost could keep a secret?"

She nodded, understanding. He took her hand back into his and they moved towards the ward. God was good, and always He walked a step ahead. They went through the door together.